SEXY STRUMPETS &
TROUBLESOME TROLLOPS

Borgo Press Books by Michael Hemmingson

Auto/Ethnographies: Sex, Death, and Symbolic Interaction
Beyond Science Fiction: Barry N. Malzberg
The Dirty Realism Duo: Charles Bukowski and Raymond Carver
The Fellowship of Amorous Gentlemen
How to Have an Affair and Other Instructions
In the Background Is a Walled City
Judas Payne
The Rose of Heaven
Seven Women: An Erotic Private Investigation
Sexy Strumpets & Troublesome Trollops: Exciting Tales (and Tails)
    of Erotic Noir
Star Trek: A Post-Structural Critique
The Stripper: A Tale of Lust and Crime
Vexatious Vixens and Trail Park Tramps
Zona Norte

FOR OTHER PRESSES

The Naughty Yard (Permeable Press, 1994)
Crack Hotel (Permeable Press, 1995)
Minstrels (Permeable Press, 1997)
The Mammoth Book of Short Erotic Novels (Carroll & Graf, 2000)
The Mammoth Book of Legal Thrillers (Carroll & Graf, 2001)
Wild Turkey (Forge, 2001)
The Comfort of Women (Blue Moon, 2002)
The Dress (Blue Moon, 2002)
My Fling with Betty Page (Eraserhead Press, 2003)
Drama (Blue Moon, 2003)
The Rooms (Blue Moon, 2003)
The Lawyer (Blue Moon, 2003)
House of Dreams Trilogy (Avalon, 2004)
The Garden of Love (Blue Moon, 2004)
Expelled from Eden: A William T. Vollmann Reader (Thunder's
    Mouth Press, 2004)
*This Other Eden (*The Dybbuk Press, 2009)
Amateurs (Olympia Press, 2009)
William T. Vollmann: A Critical Study (McFarland, 2009)
William T. Vollmann: An Annotated Bibliography (Scarecrow Press,
    2010)

SEXY STRUMPETS & TROUBLESOME TROLLOPS

ENTICING TALES (AND TAILS) OF EROTIC NOIR

by

MICHAEL HEMMINGSON

THE BORGO PRESS

An Imprint of Wildside Press LLC

MMIX

CONTENTS

For Jolene Hui, a troublesome trollop indeed

BLACKJACK WANTON

Rick, Frank, and I were at the blackjack table. The free drinks were always the best, even if they were small drinks. We were waving at the waitress a lot, demanding more.

We were having a good time.

A woman joined our table. She was in her early thirties, wore a black sweater, black skirt. She was attractive enough, a little too plenty in the rear for my tastes shoulder-length dark blonde hair. We were happy to have her join the game.

She drank as much as we did, if not more.

"I've been on a roll all night," she told us. "My luck has been real good. The money is *coming*, I can *feel* it, this is my *night.*"

She surpassed us in drinks.

She started off good, but that quickly changed. She placed high bets. We couldn't match her in both alcohol and gambler's risk.

"I'm broke," she announced, like it was a surprise.

She explored her purse, couldn't find any more money.

She had to sit the next hand out, dazed.

Frank, next to her, won the hand, bringing in eighty bucks.

She stared at his chips, licked her lips.

She leaned toward Frank, said something to him I couldn't hear. He looked at her, thinking, and nodded. He gathered his chips.

"Be back," he said, and left with the woman.

Rick and I looked at each other.

"Well, well," aid Rick.

We played several more hands. Frank and the woman came back. She had chips to play with. Frank didn't meet our eyes, went back into the game. He'd been married for seven years.

She lost all her chips immediately, reckless in her bets. She called for a drink. She leaned over to Rick and whispered to him.

He gathered his chips and left with her.

Frank and I looked at each other and Frank flushed. Rick had been married for five years.

"Well, well," I said.

Rick and the woman came back twenty minutes later. I had a new drink. She sat next to me and smiled. I smiled back. She was looking prettier every time, or maybe the booze was finally getting to me.

She lost all her chips in no time.

"Damn," she said.

She sat the next hand out.

* * * * * * *

"Twenty bucks," she said; "all I really need is twenty bucks and I just know I can get back on the right track here."

She leaned toward me and whispered something—okay, so I gathered my chips and left with her.

We went up to the fifth floor of the hotel, where she had a room. I'd been married for twelve years.

She went to the bathroom first.

I examined the room. An ordinary room, a suitcase by the bed.

She came out, fresh lipstick. "You can pay me with money or chips," she said. "Your friends just wanted blowjobs, and that's thirty. You want something else, we can negotiate. I'll do anything, doesn't matter how bizarre or kinky, as long as you have the money or chips."

I said, "You do this just to gamble?"

Must have hit some arduous in her. She began to cry. I went to her, put my arm around her shoulder. "It's okay." I felt stupid.

She wiped at her tears with an arm and smiled.

In another story, where I might have been noble, nothing would've happened. I might've even talked her out of this bad situation. But I was on vacation, I was drunk, I'd been fighting with my wife....

I gave this woman forty bucks worth of chips and she sucked my cock. The extra ten was for licking my balls a bit.

"No," she said after, "I'm not a professional whore. I have an ex-husband and kids, in a city I left months ago. I've been here ever since, drinking and gambling. Sometimes I get there, I get real *close*, and I *know* my Big Chance is coming. I have to catch it, and I'll catch it any way I can."

THE LUST SEEKERS

It was half past three P.M. in a dark bedroom inside the Sheraton Hotel, downtown Los Angeles. Outside, a storm was coming in and the air was muggy. Robert Ford and Catherine Ellison were beginning something, kissing and touching and moving toward the bed.

"Wait, stop," Catherine said.

"What?"

"I can't."

"Something is wrong," Robert said.

"I know," Catherine said. "I know."

"I don't understand," he said, "you suggested this."

"I know, I know. I'm—sorry."

"You're sorry?"

"What *more* do you want me to say?"

"I thought you wanted this."

"So did I."

"I mean, you're separated from your husband."

"I guess I'm not ready."

"An hour ago, you said you were."

"I had two drinks in me and they wore off," Catherine said, "the drinks, I mean, that feeling. You know? You don't know. I'll reimburse you for the room."

"Forget it," he said, "it's on the studio's card, a business expense. We'll call it research. Let's go," he said.

She asked, "Are you mad at me?"

"Of course not." He kissed her on the cheek.

They left the Sheraton and got into their respective cars and merged onto different L.A. freeways. There was much traffic, as always. There are too many people in L.A., Robert thought, and they're all a product of my imagination.

He called Chuck on the car phone.

"So," Chuck said. "Talk to me."

"The woman is driving me nuts."

"Nothing happened, I take it."

"I don't know what's going on in her head."

"Having regrets you hired her?"

"Not at all, she's the best actress for the part. I'm sorry I got it in my little brain that she was good for an affair."

"Maybe it wasn't the best idea," Chuck said, who was the screenwriter for the movie Robert was directing and Catherine Ellison had a minor, but integral, part in.

"Yeah, well. You got those changes done?"

"I need another day."

"One more day. We're already behind."

"Are we ever ahead?" asked Chuck.

"I have another call," Robert said.

"Later," Chuck said.

"Hey," Catherine's voice said on the other line. "Okay, are you mad at me?"

"I said I wasn't."

"I don't want to this ruin the movie."

"It won't."

"I know how much you want to have an affair," Catherine said, "so I have an idea. I'll hook you up with my friend Terri."

"Who?" he said. "Who's Terri?"

"She's separated and wants...something. Like you do."

"Who?"

"I met her at this group thing, this—you know, you sit in a circle in a room in Santa Monica and you talk about common things. Things about being married."

"Look," Robert said, "forget it."

"You'll like her."

"It's okay."

"Do this for me," Catherine said.

"Your impulses are going to drive me insane, you know," he said, "completely."

"That's what my husband always says."

Robert drove to Sherman Oaks, to the eight-bedroom house on a hill, and there in the place he called home was his wife, Sharon, sitting naked on a bean bag and reading a thick novel.

"Hello," she said.

"Hello," he said.

"This is a damn good book," she said, "you should check into getting the rights."

He looked at the cover and said, "Kitchen Creek already bought it."

"Too bad," Sharon said.

Sharon's twenty-year-old lover, Nathan, walked out of the bathroom, naked, went to fridge and got a bottled juice; he noticed Robert, smiled and said, "Hey."

"Nathan."

"Bob."

"How are you?"

"I'm okay," said Nathan, "you?"

"Well," Robert said, and opened the fridge and got himself a bottled juice.

"We didn't know you'd be home this early," Sharon said.

"Either did I."

"Weren't you supposed to screw someone?" Nathan asked.

"Oh yes," Sharon said, "that actress."

"Nothing ever works out the way you planned," Robert said.

"Ain't that true," Nathan said.

"What do *you* know?"

"I know a lot, Bob."

"He knows plenty," Sharon said.

Robert drank his juice and went upstairs to his bedroom and took a nap.

* * * * * * *

Catherine Ellison said, "May I present to you Mrs. Terri Dodd, soon to return to her maiden name, Terri Franklin."

They were in the bar at the Sheraton, each drinking a glass of wine.

"So you're getting a divorce," Robert said.

"No," Terri said, brushing a strand of red hair out of her eyes, "but I'm thinking about it."

"Aren't we all," Catherine said and laughed, nervously.

Robert looked at Catherine and Catherine stopped laughing.

"Well," Catherine said and sipped at her wine.

"So you're in the movie biz," Terri said.

"Are you an actress?" he said.

"No."

"Screenwriter?"

"No."

"Costume designer maybe?"

"She's not in the biz," Catherine said.

"So how do you two—?"

"Many years," said Terri. "Since we were in high school."

"Really?" he said.

"Really," Terri said.

"Well, here we are," Catherine said; in time she left and Robert and Terri went up to the room he'd gotten on the studio's card.

As they undressed, Terri said, "You still live with your wife?"

He said, "Yes."

She said, "I still live with my husband. Do you understand why I'm doing this?"

"I don't need to."

"I want to tell you," she said, "I want to have an affair because I've never done anything like this. I just turned thirty and I've been married for ten years and seven of those years have not been good. I haven't been happy in seven years."

"Thirty? You're young."

"How old are you?"

"Thirty-eight."

"When I was fifteen," she said, "I slept with one of my teachers, he was thirty-three. I thought he was ancient."

"Sometimes I feel ancient," Robert said. "When I turned thirty I slept with a fifteen-year-old actress at Disney because I thought it would make me feel young again."

"Did it?"

"Yes."

"What does your wife do?"

"She sleeps with boys."

They had sex and while they had sex Terri said, "I wanted to have an affair so I could feel alive."

"Do you feel alive?" he asked her.

She said she did and he said he did and when it was all over they both felt happy.

* * * * * * *

A few weeks later, Catherine called him on the cell phone and said, "I need to see you right now, *right now.*"

"What's wrong?" Robert asked.

"Please," she said.

He met her on Mulholland Drive, parked his car behind hers. Catherine got into his car, wearing a short blue dress and sandals.

"Okay," he said, "I'm here."

"I can't deal with this."

"Catherine," he said, "what? The movie? There's some snags, but this movie *will* happen."

"Are you and Terri falling in love?"

"Why do you ask?"

"Tell me," she said.

"Ask Terri."

"I did."

"And what did she say?"

"She said it wasn't my business."

"Maybe it isn't."

"Don't give me that," said Catherine Ellison, "don't give me *that*. I hooked you two up."

"Yes you did."

"I've known her forever."

"Yes you have."

"So I have the right to know."

"No you don't."

"Goddamn you."

"I don't get it, Cat."

She pulled her dress up; she wasn't wearing underwear and she said, "Do you like what you see?"

"You shave," he said, looking.

"Do you want it?"

"That's a funny question."

They kissed and touched each other.

She said, "I don't want to go to that stupid hotel."

"Where? Here? In the car? Like teenagers?"

"My place."

"I thought you never wanted me to—"

"A woman can change her mind," she said.

They drove both cars down the hill to North Hollywood. Her apartment was very small and he was surprised. She had a waterbed. They undressed and got on the waterbed and kissed and touched and then Catherine said, "Wait, stop."

"What?"

"I can't."

"Holy cow," Robert said, and he stood up and started to get dressed. "I can't deal with this again, Cat," he said, "I can't do this anymore."

"You don't understand," she said.

"No," he said, "I don't, and to be quite frank, my dear, I don't want to."

"I want to sleep with you," she said, "I have ever since we met, but—every time—what I mean—look—"

"What?"

"Someone tried to rape me."

"What? When?"

"Recently."

"When?"

"Two months ago."

"Who?"

"Chuck."

"Chuck?"

"Yeah."

"No."

"Yes."

"No."

"I said yes."

"When?"

"I said two months ago."

"I don't get it."

"Oh, Robert. *I'm in love with you.* Don't fall in love with Terri. That was supposed to be a diversion."

"Chuck *raped* you?"

"Well," Catherine said, "he tried."

"He 'tried'?"

"That's what I said."

"I don't understand what that means."

"It means he tried, and then I ran away."

"You ran?"

"I ran fast."

"But he recommended you," Robert said.

"Yeah," she said, "he did."

Robert was dressed now and he was determined to get to the bottom of this so he drove to Chuck's apartment, which wasn't too far away in Silverlake.

It was almost midnight and Chuck was busy at his laptop working on an episode for a sit-com starring Robert Downey, Jr. as well as a poem for literary purposes and a chapter on a "serious" novel he'd been laboring on for six years and drinking vodka with Diet Pepsi Vanilla; needless to say, he was surprised to see the director of his current film script at the door—looking haggard, disoriented and confused.

"Bob," Chuck said.

Robert socked him in the nose. Chuck stumbled back, touching his nose, which was bleeding.

"What the fuck," said Chuck.

"You raped Cat."

"I did not."

"She said—"

"Reality," said Chuck, "eludes that wonderfully beautiful woman."

* * * * * * *

The two men—two old friends—sat down with a couple of beers and talked. Chuck held a towel stuffed with ice to his nose.

"When I first met Catherine Ellison," Chuck said, "not only did I know she was perfect for the part you cast her in, I knew I had to have her. That's what I told myself anyway. 'I have to have her.' So I asked her out."

"Wait," said Robert, "where did you meet—"

"Where else," said Chuck, "she was in one of my plays."

"A *play*?"

"I also write plays."

"Yes, yes, of course."

"She was in my little play at that one-act festival—the Venice Beach Fringe Festival."

"I missed that."

"Yeah, tell me about."

"So you met her—"

"I met her there and I asked her out and she said she was married, then later she said so what, she's married but separated, so we go out, we go to her studio apartment, we're getting into things, and then suddenly she starts crying and going, 'Rape rape.'"

"What?"

"That's what I said. She tells me she can't do it. She tells me she met this guy at a class, a scene or acting class, it was the goddamn Mesiner Technique—"

"So what happened?"

"She went to this guy's place, the ruse was a copy of a scene or exercise in dialogue she missed because she missed a class, and this guy tried to do the nasty."

"He—"

"He tried to force her—"

"He raped her?"

"He tried, but she got away."

"I'm lost," Robert said. "She told me it was you."

"We've known each other for a number of years, Bob."

"Yeah."

"Do I do shit like that?"

"Oh boy," said Robert, "oh no."

"Yeah."

"Why didn't you tell me this about her? Why did you—"

"She was perfect for the part, and you know this is true," Chuck said, looking at the blood on the towel. "As for, well...look, Bob, she asked me not to say anything. She said you were the kind of man she could fall in love with."

"And you believed that?"

"She seemed sincere at the time."

Robert apologized and Chuck apologized and the two men shook hands. Robert then drove to Catherine's apartment and when he saw her, he held her and kissed her and then he pushed her away and said, "You not only drive me crazy, but others too. What about your husband?"

"He hates me," she said.

"Why?"

"I don't blame him, the poor soul."

"Chuck didn't rape you."

"No."

"Then why did you say that?"

"I was confused, but I'm thinking clearly now."

"Tell me about the fellow at the acting class," Robert said.

"Yes, he tried to rape me."

"Is this true?"

"Very."

"Why didn't you go to the police?"

"I did," she said. "They gave me this equipment, to record phone conversations. They told me to get him on the phone, act like nothing happened—like it was all a misunderstanding—and get him to admit it. But he knew what was going on. He had one prior rape conviction, he did a few years in prison, and there were some charges that went nowhere, so he knew what to do, I mean when I talked to him he referred tom himself in the third person and avoided any discussion about what happened between us, so when I turned the tapes in to the cops, they said: 'There's nothing we can do.'"

"And?"

"And I have a hard time being intimate now. Whenever I get close to a man, what happened with the bastard pops up in my head—"

"And now you think every many wants to hurt you?"

"Yes."

"I hurt Chuck."

"I love you."

"No you don't."

"Of course I do."

"I love Terri," he said.

"I was afraid of that," she said.

Robert drove home to Sherman Oaks. His wife, Sharon, and her lover, Nathan, were drinking $200 bottles of champagne and dancing in the living room to pretty electronic music. They were half naked—Sharon wore a black bra and Nathan wore a purple tank-top.

"Hey," he said, "what's up?"

"Wonderful news, baby!" Sharon said, holding up her champagne glass. "I'm knocked-up!"

"What?"

"Preggers!"

"We're having a baby," Nathan said, holding up his champagne glass.

"Bobby, isn't that the best news?" his wife asked.

"Yes," he said, "I suppose it is."

Sharon poured him some champagne and he tried to dance but couldn't, so he let his wife and her lover dance and thought about his first wife, who wanted a baby very badly, and how the doctor told him—at the age of twenty-two—his sperm were defective.

* * * * * * *

Five months later, as the film was shooting, Catherine Ellison went to visit her long time friend Terri Franklin; Terri had an apartment in Century City and Robert was there and when Robert saw Catherine he said, "Well." He said, "Cat," but he saw Cat every day on the set, her name was on the call sheet and she ate a lot of red seedless grapes in her trailer.

"You two look happy," Catherine said, "and that's nice."

"I feel happy," said Terri.

"That's nice. I want to be happy."

"You *should* be happy."

"I am not."

"You *deserve* to be happy."

"No she doesn't," said Robert.

"Oh don't be mean," Terri said.

"It's okay," Catherine said.

"He loves you, you know," Terri said.

"No, he loves you," Catherine said.

Robert said, "Why are you here?"

Catherine said, "I'm not sure."

Terri said, "Don't be mean, Bobby."

"It's all right," Catherine said.

"Not it isn't," Terri said.

"It is," Robert said.

"No it isn't," Terri said.

"Yes it is," Catherine said, "I have it coming."

* * * * * * *

They watched a movie on Pay-Per-View starring Vincent D'Onfrio; that's when things started to happen. They had a few White Russians while watching the wide screen. It started with Terri playing with Catherine's hair; it was an innocent gesture, really, the sort of things women do sometimes. Or so Robert thought. The petting between the women started to get heavy, and they began to kiss. Robert knew they'd done this before, maybe years and years ago, when they were girls and drunk and being experimental.

Terri turned to Robert and said, "Do you want to join us?"

He sipped his White Russian.

"Oh man," Catherine said, blushing, "I can't believe I'm doing this but it is very nice."

"Yes it's nice," Terri said, "and Bobby should join."

"Oh man," Catherine said, brushing the hair out of her eyes, "it's been so long since I've had sex."

"It's okay," Terri said.

"Will it be okay?" Catherine asked.

"It'll be very nice," Terri said.

Robert started with Catherine's toes; for months he'd wanted to be close to her feet and now the chance was here, so he sucked and nibbled on her toes and licked her feet and Catherine giggled and rolled her eyes as Terri undressed her.

In bed, he watched the two women for a while, joined in, kissed and touched them both all over, went down on each, made love to Terri, watched them make love, and then he had sex with Catherine.

Finally.

Catherine held out her arms and said to him, "Mount me."

He thought that was funny.

Something in Terri changed. She left the bed and stood against the wall, her arms crossed.

She started to get dressed.

"What's wrong?" Catherine said.

"Hey," Robert said.

"I want a drink but we're out of vodka, I'll go get some vodka," Terri said and snapped her bra in the front, "I'll just go down to the liquor store and get a fifth of Stoli," putting on a yellow silk blouse, "I won't be gone long, I'll be right back, you two just go back to your thing, I'll be back in ten, no five minutes; I'll be back and I'll have vodka."

"And you'll watch?" Robert asked.

"Yes," Terri said, "I'll watch."

Terri left. Robert and Catherine looked at each other.

"Do you think everything is all right with her?" Catherine asked.

"I'm sure it is," he said, "she just wants vodka."

"I want this to be all right," Catherine said.

"So do I."

"I've been wanting this to happen."

"I've been waiting," he said.

"This has to be okay with her."

"Don't worry."

"And it's okay with you?"

"It's not me," he said, "it's you."

"I'm happy we're doing this," Catherine said.

* * * * * * *

Terri was crying as she drove her Lexus to the liquor store. Because she was upset and in tears, she (a) didn't notice the street light was red and (b) didn't hear the siren of the police car—or even see the police car—so she smashed into the side of the LAPD cruiser and the whole matter was just one big ugly mess.

* * * * * * *

Terri was confused for several minutes. Her car wasn't moving. There was blood in her eyes because her forehead had smashed into the windshield. Her body was numb and throbbing. She freed herself from the seatbelt and thought: My airbag didn't work. She was going to have to sue somebody. She got out of the car and almost fell on her face, she was dizzy and the air smelled like gasoline. There was no one on the street except for the two cars that had collided. It was later than she thought.

She wasn't dizzy anymore and she looked at the police cruiser a hundred feet in front of her: it was upside down and the lights were still flashing and the siren kept going in and out—and then it let out one long mewl and died.

A police officer with short blonde hair and a large belly was on the ground, lying on his back and groaning.

"Help," Terri said and it was faint; she had no voice and there was no one to help. She needed to find a phone. Why didn't she bring her cell with her?

Someone was getting out of the back of the police car—he was crawling, he was handcuffed. He was tall and thin and had long red hair and there was a piece of glass in his left eye.

He crawled to the cop, pushing his back against the cop's body. Terri watched as the tall man with long red hair grabbed the cop's keys and the tall man with long red hair freed himself from the cuffs, stood up, cracked his neck, shook his arms, reached down and took the cop's gun—a 9mm Glock—and shot the cop twice.

Terri jumped at each shot.

The man turned and looked at her.

She wanted to run but she could not run.

He pointed the gun at her.

With his other hand, he removed the piece of glass from his eye and tossed the piece of glass to the ground.

He walked toward her.

"Stay where you are," he said.

"Don't hurt me," she said.

"Be good and I won't," he said, and now he was standing right in front of her. "What's your name?"

She closed her eyes.

He pressed the gun to her forehead and said, "Look at me and tell me your goddamn name."

She opened her eyes and told him.

"Well, Terri," he said, "my name is Frank."

She just looked at him and she started to shake.

"This isn't the best situation to meet a new person," Frank said, "and we have to get out of here. Your car doesn't look in too bad shape. It can still run. I bet it can still run. We need to go. *C'mon, Terri, we need to go.*"

They got into the Lexus. Frank sat next to her and held the gun to her side.

The car started but it sounded bad. The car moved but steam and smoke began to rise from the engine, and the smell of gasoline got stronger. After two blocks, the car died. They were on a side street and it was dark.

"This is okay," Frank said, and looked at her with his one good eye. "You're one hot bitch," he said, "one hot rich bitch in a nice car who crashed into the wrong pig at the wrong time with the wrong prisoner."

Terri said, "Please."

Frank said, "Please what? Please don't fuck you? Oh, you got my dick hard already, girl."

After he raped her, they sat there and didn't look at each other. Frank seemed just as disgusted with what happened as she was.

"I can never do anything right," Frank said.

There was the sound of distant sirens, many of them.

"They're coming," Frank said. "We can't hang out here. As much as I'd like to, we gotta go."

They left the car and began to walk.

"Where do you live, Terri?" Frank asked. "And don't lie to me. I'll know if you're lying. If you lie, I'll put a couple of bullets in you like I did to that pig."

"Not far," she said. "Three blocks."

"Good. We'll go to your place."

"And then you'll kill me?"

"I don't want to kill you," he said. "I'm not as bad as you think."

They walked.

"Why were you arrested?" she asked.

"I robbed a liquor store about forty minutes ago," he said.

"Why?"

"Why do you think, rich bitch? I need money."

"I'm not rich."

"Your life is better than mine."

"Don't be so sure."

"Terri," he said, "stop."

She stopped.

"Look at me now."

She turned around.

"Tell me a secret," he said. "Tell me a dark secret that no one else in the world knows."

"Why?"

"Just do it."

"I guess I don't have a choice," she said.

He lowered the gun.

"Before it's too late," he said.

"The man I love, he's with another woman right now," she said. "She loves him, and he loves her. They really didn't know this about each other until tonight, but somehow I knew, I knew in my heart, it was bound to happen sooner or…sooner or something."

"The bastard is cheating on you?"

"No."

"Who is this other woman?"

"My best friend," Terri said. "I also love her."

"I would like to meet them and tell them how dumb they are," Frank said. "You're a beautiful woman and when I had you…We share things now, Terri."

"Tell me a secret, Frank."

He nodded and said, "Fair enough. The robbery tonight, I screwed it up on purpose. I wanted to be caught."

"Why?"

"I have nothing. I don't have a place to sleep because I got kicked out of my motel room two nights ago. I don't have a dime to my name. In jail, I can sleep on a cot and get food. I know that probably sounds weird to you but that's the way it is."

"So what changed your mind?" she asked. "Why did you kill that officer and why are you—"

"I changed my mind about everything when I saw you," he said. They walked.

"How's your eye?" Terri said. "It doesn't look good."

"I'll be okay. Thanks for asking."

* * * * * * *

Robert and Catherine didn't hear anything, they were too busy having sex. Terri and Frank watched them for about a minute and then Frank said, "Well, isn't this special."

Robert jumped up. Catherine made a small and horrible noise, and another when she saw the gun and the look on Terri's face.

Robert was on his feet and saying, "What the hell is going on here," when Frank shot him three times in the chest.

Catherine covered her mouth and her eyes were wide.

"I don't like naked men talking to me," Frank said. "It's like the faggots in jail."

"I thought you wanted to go to jail," Terri said softly.

"Faggots are the worst part of jail," Frank said, "except for maybe the straight guys who fuck other guys just for the fun of it."

"He's—dead," Catherine mumbled, looking at Robert's body.

"He's a dead one, and I did it for you," Frank said to Terri, "I did it for you because he broke your heart."

"You didn't do it for me, Frank. Don't lie to me. You did because you like it."

"No, no," and Frank shook his head, "I don't like killing, girl."

"Terri?" said Catherine Ellison.

"Is this her?" Frank said. "Is this the best friend you told me about?"

Terri looked at Catherine and said, "Yes."

"Do you want me to kill her, too?"

"No."

"Terri?" said Catherine.

"Hasn't she broken your heart?" Frank asked.

"I broke my own heart."

"You said you love her, is this true?"

Terri's eyes were locked on Catherine. "Yes, Frank, it is very true."

"Good. Because this is what's gonna happen. I wanna show, a lesbian feast. I wanna see you naked with her. I wanna see you go down on her. I wanna see you *fuck her* like you love her."

"You're not getting a show, Frank," said Terri, "wasn't violating me enough for you?"

"This could be the last night of my life and it has to be a memorable one, you know what I mean?" he said.

She said, "I know what you mean."

"So get naked and get with your best friend here."

Catherine said, "Terri?"

Terri said, "It'll be all right."

Frank said, "It'll all be just fine."

Terri said, "I won't do it, Frank."

Frank pointed the gun at Catherine and said, "I'll shoot her then. You know I will."

Terri started to unbutton her blouse.

"Oh my God, Terri," Catherine said and started to cry.

"Hush now," Frank said.

Then: the sound of sirens.

The sirens were getting louder, closer.

"Oh shit," Frank said softly. "They know I'm here, don't they?"

Terri said, "People probably saw us walking, you had that gun to my back, I have nosey neighbors."

"Shit."

"It is the last night of your life, Frank."

"I'll go down in a blaze of glory and bullets," he said, "and I have two pretty hostages to keep the wolves away from the door—for a while."

"I set the silent alarm off when we came inside," Terri said, "you fucking idiot."

She was surprised how fast and easy it was. She grabbed Frank's arm and pointed it up. The gun fired. She kneed him in the groin. He went down in pain. She had the Glock. She pointed it at him and stepped back.

Frank looked up and said, "You don't know how to shoot that."

"How hard can it be," Terri said, "all you have to do is pull," and she put the rest of the bullets into his body: four in all.

* * * * * * *

Sharon and Nathan saw it on the morning news, three hours after the police came by.

"It's true," Nathan said, "it's on TV."

"Robert," Sharon said, touching her pregnant belly.

"Oh man, *it's true,*" Nathan said, pacing back and forth, "I don't know how to deal with this, I've never known anyone who was murdered."

"He'll come back, he'll reincarnate," Sharon said with a soothing voice.

"Yeah? You into that stuff?"

"I know it," she said, "because his soul will be inside our baby."

"Yeah? How?"

"That's the way we reincarnate, honey; our souls jump into new baby bodies."

Nathan knelt and placed his head against Sharon's belly. "Bob, that you in there? Hello, Bob? How can you be so sure it's Bob?" he asked.

"I felt him go in last night," said Sharon, smiling, "I feel him inside me right now."

THE SIN SEEKERS

"I don't mind a reasonable amount of trouble."
                    —Sam Spade in *The Maltese Falcon*

1.

I was close to thirty and things weren't going good for me; they hadn't for a long time.

On my twenty-ninth birthday, I drove from Los Angeles to Las Vegas in my crappy station wagon. I was divorced, alone, without any prospects; I had some money from stock options and figured I might as well piss it all away.

In a traffic jam on the Strip, I rear-ended a black Cadillac. A large, muscular bald man in a neon green suit got out. He looked pissed-off.

"Oh shit," I said.

I couldn't drive anywhere to escape.

The big man in green opened my door and yanked me out. He smashed my face onto the hood. I tasted blood.

"Bitch," he said, "I'm gonna kill you."

I heard a gun shot.

I wasn't the one shot.

The big man stepped back, touching the bleeding bullet hole in his side.

"Leon—in—neon!" a Rastafarian with plenty of long dirty dreds said. He was standing on the sidewalk, dressed in white leather. He was holding a handgun with a silencer.

No one on the Strip paid attention except me.

"Bitch," Leon in neon green said, "you shot me."

"Yah, and I's gonna shoot you again, mon."

The Rasta guy did just that, shooting Leon in neon three times in the chest.

Leon went down.

Red blood, like the blood that would be on my windshield a few days later.

Rasta pointed his gun at me.

"I don't know him," I said.

"I just saved your life." Rasta smiled, his gun down. "One of these days, you owe me, mon. Be ready for that day."

He turned, and walked away very fast.

There was a break in the traffic. I jumped into my car and got the hell out of there.

I went straight to the Stardust Hotel and checked into a room.

2.

What I needed was a massage and a blowjob. I looked in the Vegas Yellow Pages and called Dial A Perky Blonde.

I gave my Visa Card number over the phone. It was a new card with plenty of credit.

There was still blood in my mouth. I checked for missing teeth. There were a few loose ones, but I knew they'd hold in there.

The escort arrived forty minutes later. She was nineteen or twenty; blonde and perky. The hair on her head was too blonde. Her tits were small and perky. Her body and voice were also—perky.

"So," she said, "so, so, so."

"A massage," I said, "and then I'd like you to suck my dick."

"Three hundred."

"Two."

"Deal!"

"I want you to eat my cum, too."

"You're crazy," she said, "that will cost you an extra hundred—and I won't swallow it. I'll hold it in my mouth. But I'm spitting it in the sink. The world's just too dangerous to be eating the cum of strangers."

"A hundred bucks," I said, "forget it."

She shrugged.

"And I'm not wearing a condom," I said, "I don't want a blow-job with a condom, I mean what's the point?"

"No condom, an extra fifty."

"Deal."

When she left, I went down to the casino and played some blackjack.

* * * * * * *

I left Vegas with two hundred and three dollars more to my name than I'd arrived with. This was a good sign. This was a turning point. The drive back to L.A. was pleasant.

On the freeway, I called my friend Sammy on the cell phone.

"Riker!" he said.

"Sammy."

"Hey, hey, hey," said Sammy.

"I'm feeling good," I told him, "I'm feeling *real* good."

"Me too," said Sammy. "I had this great XTC last night. Not in a pill. Powder. You snort it. And—"

"You don't understand," I said, "I'm *feeling* good. No bipolar shit here. I'm feeling—positive."

He said, "Adrian is having a party tonight."

"Yeah?"

"You should go."

"I think I will."

"See you there?"

"See you there," I said, and pressed the "End" button on the cell.

He didn't even say happy birthday. Well, I didn't tell him, and I didn't expect him to know. We weren't good friends.

I had no friends, really.

3.

Adrian's party in Santa Monica was infested with a lot of Los Angeles wannabes: indie film actors, sit-com extras, theater throw-aways, budding screenwriters bullshitting about their first sale around the corner, neophyte directors who couldn't find their way out of their own assholes without a guide-dog.

The usual riff-raff.

But there I was, in fresh clothes, showered, drink in hand, chatting away with these folks. I had the smile on my face. You learn the L.A. smile fast if you want to maintain idle party-talk.

I was making myself a second drink—I was drinking Long Island Iced Teas—when I ran into Sammy.

"Come with me," he said.

I followed him into the bathroom. He had a vial in his hand. He poured some powder onto the basin and started cutting up lines.

"Wait," I said, "that isn't the snortable XTC you were talking about, is it?" I wasn't in the mood for E.

"Nah, it's blow."

"Okay."

Sammy handed me a rolled up fifty dollar bill. I bent down and snorted a line off the sink. When I stood, I looked at my reflection in the mirror. Thin long hair, a beard. Twenty-nine years old and going nowhere, but I knew that was all about to change.

"What do you think?" Sammy asked.

"It's good."

"Better than usual."

A young lady in a thin emerald dress opened the bathroom door. "Ooops," she said. "I just wanted to pee." She saw the coke. "Hey, can I join?"

"Sure," Sammy said, handing her the bill.

She bent and snorted. She smelled nice, and she smelled like trouble. I decided to leave her and Sammy alone.

I had been married to a woman like the young woman in the emerald dress—the aspiring actress/model/singer/artist who loves her drugs. I was in the rut that I was in because of that marriage.

I felt something bad in my gut. The coke was making my scalp tingle.

I didn't want to be around these people anymore. I loathed these people. I fucking hated every one of them and what they stood for and all their crap and it seemed like I just couldn't get away from them; this was L.A. and there was just no getting away from them. I told myself long ago that I would stop coming to these parties.

I could get away from them now. I could take action and just leave. So what if I'd only been here for half an hour? Who would notice? Who would care? I'd rather be alone.

I left the party. I got into my car and drove home.

I was on Wilshire ten minutes later. There was a lot of traffic but traffic was moving fast and steady.

I turned on the radio.

Something jumped in front of my car. A large object. I thought someone had thrown something at my car. I hit the object with a thud. My windshield cracked. The object flew away. I kept driving. I was driving faster. What the fuck was that? There was blood on my windshield. Did I hit something that was alive? It was awfully big. Was it a person? Did I hit a person?

I turned around at the first light. I had to go back and find out what that was.

Traffic was at a still up ahead. People were gathering. On the street lay the body of a woman with dark skin—a tan, I think, or was that just the blood? She wore a dress and a coat. Her body was twisted. I'd hit her with my car all right. What was she doing in the middle of Wilshire and Santa Monica where there was no cross-walk?

I turned my car around, took a side road, and got the hell out of there.

I don't know what I was thinking. I *wasn't* thinking.

4.

I parked my car at my apartment building. I inspected the vehicle—evidence of the impact was on the hood: a dent, more blood. *Blood on the windshield.*

I was fucked, and it wasn't sinking in how *really* fucked I was, and how badly I had just fucked up.

I went up to my apartment and tried to think of whom I could call about this. Like I said, I had no friends.

I called my step-father in Palm Springs. That bastard would get a kick out of this. He didn't answer the phone, and I didn't leave a message.

I'd just returned to L.A. and now I had to leave again. There wasn't anything else I could do.

I packed some clothes.

I grabbed a spare towel.

I returned to my car. I looked around, made sure no one was watching. I was alone. I cleaned some of the blood off the hood and the windshield.

I tossed the towel into the trunk. I'd get rid of it somewhere, anywhere.

I got back into my car and drove.

I kept thinking of the excuses I'd make if a cop stopped me and wanted to know about my cracked windshield. "A rock from a bridge," I'd say, "I parked the car in West Hollywood and went to a club and when I came out, there was the cracked windshield. Must have been some kids. An ex-girlfriend did it, she's jealous, should I put a restraining order on her?"

I hadn't been pulled over by the cops since I was nineteen.

I got on the freeway and headed for Palm Springs.

5.

There wasn't enough gas in my tank to make it all the way. I could have stopped for gas, and I would have made it to my step-father's house; but this didn't happen.

I was *in* Palm Springs, at least. My car died about three miles from my step-father's.

I left the car on the side of the road and walked. It was actually nice to walk in the Palm Springs night; this gave me time to calm down and think.

By the time I arrived at my step-father's house, my feet hurt and the sun was beginning to rise.

I wasn't ready for a new day. I had no choice.

I thought of calling him first, but the battery had run out on the cell phone.

I sat on the curb in front of my step-father's house and took my shoes off. My socks were sweaty and stank. My body stank. I wanted to lay in a bed and sleep for a long time.

The birds were chirping.

A kid on a bicycle rode by, and tossed the morning paper on the lawn. The kid looked at me. I smiled and said good morning but he didn't say anything, just rode away and kept tossing papers around the neighborhood.

I heard a door open behind me. I stood up. My step-father still rose at dawn, and read the paper. I'm sure he still drank a whole pot of coffee while doing so. He was wearing an old worn black robe. I knew that robe from childhood. He was bald, and wore gold-rimmed glasses.

"Bill," I said.

He looked at me and squinted. "Robert?"

I walked toward him, holding my shoes. "How you doing? Good morning. I mean hello. I mean, I know this must seem weird."

"It's unexpected. What kind of trouble you in, kid?"

"Trouble?"

"You look like shit," he said. "You look like you've been through hell. You look like you're in trouble."

"Yeah," I said. "I am."

"You got that same look on your face like when you were a kid—like when you'd get in trouble."

"Can I come inside?"

* * * * * * *

He offered me a cup of coffee. I sat at the small table in the dining room. The TV was on, CNN. He was always a news junkie. He'd never gone anywhere in the world, but he liked to know about the world.

I told him about my car running out of gas and that I walked the three miles to get here.

"I haven't seen you in five years," he said. "Since your mother passed away."

When my mother died, he took the insurance money and moved to Palm Springs. I'd gotten some money, but blew it within eight months.

"I know," I said, knowing what he was getting at.

"I get a phone call—what? Christmas? Father's Day? Not even Father's Day. My birthday? No. Christmas. Once a year. 'Merry Christmas, Bill.' 'Merry Christmas, kid.'"

"Bill," I said.

"And now here you are."

"Bill," I said.

"You say you're in trouble, and you show up at my door at six-thirty in the morning."

"Bill," I said. "Look—"

"Is it money? Do you need money? I can give you some money. Not a lot, but I can give you some money if you need money because I know how it goes, I was your age once, I was poor, I know how it goes when you need money."

"It's not money."

"What is it?"

I told him about the car accident last night.

"Shit," he said, and sipped his coffee. He shook his head. "You did a hit and run."

"I didn't want to. I went back. There were people there—"

"But you left. It's still a hit and run."

"I got scared. I wasn't thinking. I'd been at a party."

"*And* you were partying?"

"A little."

"So what are you going to do?"

"I don't know."

"Why did you come here? Do you think I know what to do?"

"I didn't know who I could talk to," I said. "I didn't know what I should do."

He sighed and shook his head. "The first thing you need to do is go get your car. I have a five gallon gas tank in the garage. Wait. Before that, go take a shower. You smell."

I showered. My step-father was dressed and ready to go. We took his Dodge truck: a big, green ugly thing he'd had since I was ten years old. We stopped at the gas station, I filled the five gallon tank.

6.

There were two sheriff cruisers parked next to my car. There were three sheriffs standing around, looking at it.

"Oh shit," I said.

My step-father drove by the scene.

"Don't look at them," he said.

I didn't. Out of the corner of my eye, I could see one of the sheriffs looking at us.

"I'll take the next street up here," my step-father said, "and we'll go back home. Obviously, we need to come up with a new plan."

"Yeah," I said.

"You really fucked up this time, kid," he said.

"Yeah," I said.

7.

Back at his house, I thanked my step-father for not stopping his truck.

"What," he said, sitting down in his chair, "you think I'd turn you in? Maybe I haven't seen you for a while, maybe we didn't get along the best when I was married to your mother, maybe you're not my real flesh and blood, but I'd never turn a guy in to the cops. I hate the fucking cops like anyone else. I've had my run in with the law when I was your age, younger too, I did a little jail time, I don't trust the system or cops for anything. What I think you're going to need at this point," he said, "is a lawyer."

"I was thinking that too."

"Know any?"

"No."

"I know one here. We'll call him at ten. I have an idea." He looked around, found the TV remote, turned the TV on. He changed channels to an L.A. station, morning news. "Let's see if you made the TV headlines, boy. Let's see if you're famous."

Forty minutes later, the blonde anchorwoman mentioned a Russian woman getting hit by a car on Wilshire last night. She was working at a nearby retail store, had just gotten off work. The car that hit her left the scene of the accident. Eye witness reports were sketchy, it was dark. "Los Angeles Police say that the driver probably won't be charged with vehicular manslaughter, as the Russian woman was illegally crossing the street—unless the driver was under the influence," the anchorwoman said. "The driver will be charged with felony hit and run."

I felt like I was going to be sick.

"Well, there's something, at least," my step-father said.

* * * * * * *

My step-father got ahold of the lawyer he knew. I talked to the lawyer on the phone. I told him what happened, about the sheriffs at my car. He said he'd look into it and call back.

He called back two hours later. He said to come into his office after lunch.

8.

The lawyer's name was Kurt O'Brien. He was a single-attorney outfit, one secretary, a small office downtown Palm Springs. He was in his fifties and heavy-set, slicked-back silver hair, patchy skin. I wondered how my step-father knew him.

My step-father drove me to the lawyer's office, and sat there with me as O'Brien gave me the "scoop."

"The sheriff made a routine stop to check out your wheels. Abandoned car, you know. Noticed the cracked windshield, the dent on the hood. And blood. There was plenty of blood on your car, Mr. Riker."

"How do you know all this, Kurt?" my step-father asked.

"The cops told me."

"Did you tell them you knew who I was?" I said nervously.

"I told them I was representing your interests."

I didn't feel good.

O'Brien smiled. "Relax. I'm a *lawyer.*"

"It's okay," my step-father told me, a hand on my shoulder.

"They ran your plates," O'Brien continued, "get an L.A. address, your name, your car matches a description of a hit and run. All they need to do is match the blood on your car to the woman. But you did run the woman over."

"Yeah," I said.

"I called the LAPD. They shuffle me to some detective, nice guy. He says you won't be charged with vehicular manslaughter."

"That's what the news said," I said.

"Unless you were under the influence."

My voice lowered. "We have a problem there."

"Were you drunk?"

"He was at a party," my step-father said.

"A party? For how long?"

"Not long," I said.

"Did you drink?"

"I had two drinks."

"Beers? Cocktails?"

"Long Island Iced Teas."

He whistled. "Strong stuff. What are you, five-ten?"

"Yeah."

"Weight?"

"One-eighty."

"You may or may not have been over the legal limit. Doesn't matter, that's moot. But hear me and hear me well: do *not*, and I repeat *not*, tell anyone, ever, outside this office, and especially not to the police or the D.A., that you had two of these Long Island Ices Teas. Do you understand me?"

"Yes," I said.

"What about drugs? Did you do any drugs at this party?"

"Yes."

"Oh, shit, Robert," my step-father said.

O'Brien held up a hand. "What kind of drugs? Pot?"

"Cocaine," I said. "Just one line."

"One line is enough to get you seven years in prison, Robert Riker. If they know about it. I was going to suggest you and I go down to the sheriff's station so you can turn yourself in. That's now changed. Coke is detectible in your system for at least 72 hours. The booze we don't have to worry about, that's already out. Should I go on?"

"Yes," I said.

"You need to lay low for, oh, let's say four more days. Make it five, to be safe. Can he stay at your place, Bill?" he asked my step-father.

"Sure. Why not."

"Good. Five days, you turn yourself in. I'll be there with you. I'll tell them I'm bringing you in. But here's the other thing: you *don't* tell them you were at a party. You don't tell them anything. We'll say you were just driving around, clearing your head, who knows, people drive in L.A. for many reasons. But no party. Why? The L.A. D.A. will want to know where this party was, whose party. Your friends will be questioned, subpoenaed. Someone might say they saw you drinking, they saw you doing the blow. That won't be good. At no time do we want the D.A. to think you were under the influence. You'll just be charged with the hit and run."

"Will I go to jail?"

"It's a felony...have you ever been convicted of anything?"

"I've never been arrested," I said.

"There was that shop-lifting shit when you were fifteen," my step-father said.

"He was a minor, that's expunged," O'Brien said. "So, nothing? Nothing at all?"

"Traffic tickets," I said.

"For what?"

"Running a stop sign, not having my seat belt on."

"That's nothing. Okay, you have a clean record. You won't do any time, not major time. Maybe a little time, maybe some community service. You'll get a slap on the wrist we play this right, okay? This could be worse, but I'm on the job, okay?"

"Okay."

"But here's the other thing—I'll handle the matter here in Palm Springs. It's better you turn yourself in here, since your car is here. You go back to L.A., the sheriff here will get pissed. The sheriff will think you were here, then you split. He might put things together and give your old man a hard time, and we don't want that."

"No," my step-father said, "we *don't* want that."

"No," I agreed. I knew I was being a pain-in-the-ass enough for him.

"You're arrested here, they'll transport you to L.A. I know a good lawyer in L.A., he'll do right by you."

"Okay," I said.

"Now we need to talk about money," O'Brien said. "My normal retainer is a thousand dollars, then one hundred fifty an hour. Seeing that you're Bob's kid and all, and Bob is a friend, I'll just charge you five hundred bucks; that'll cover all the running around on the phone and my time down at the sheriff station when it comes. Okay?"

"Okay," I said, and reached for my checkbook. I wondered what the lawyer in L.A. would cost me. It was a good thing I didn't lose my savings in Las Vegas.

9.

The next five days, I slept on the couch at my step-father's. He didn't seem to mind. It was uncomfortable—being here, being near him. There may have been a time when we were close, but it seemed like another life. We were close when I was a child; that changed when I became a teenager. We were close when my mother died five years ago, and that was brief, the way people get close when someone they love dies of cancer.

10.

O'Brien accompanied me to the Palm Springs Police Station. My step-father didn't want to be there. He said being around cops made his stomach turn. I knew what he meant.

I turned myself in.

I was arrested, and processed.

I was placed in a holding cell with several other men. I didn't talk to anyone. I was given a sandwich and an apple to eat.

I had to give up my clothes for a dark blue jail outfit.

In the morning, I was transported to the court in Indio. I was to be remanded to the Los Angeles County Sheriff's department for arraignment.

"No bail?" I asked O'Brien.

"Not until you get to L.A.," he said. "Don't worry. My friend in L.A. will help you."

11.

Two days later, I was paid a visit by one Max Waxman, a criminal defense attorney with a Beverly Hills office. Looking at his slick suit, I knew this was going to cost me every penny I had in the bank.

We sat in the attorney-client conference room in the L.A. courthouse downtown.

"How you doing, Robert? It *is* Robert? Bob? Bobby?"

"Robert."

"How you doing?"

"I want to get the fuck out of here," I said, and I meant it.

"L.A. County jail is no picnic, I know."

"You've been in jail?"

"No." He smiled. "But many of my clients have. So let's get down to business."

"What is this going to cost me?"

"My fee will be a clean three grand if we clear this matter up today in court. Can you handle that?"

"I can. We're not going to trial?"

"Do you want to go to trial?" he asked.

"I don't want to go to prison," I replied.

He nodded. "You won't have to. You're not being charged with vehicular manslaughter. The woman had no business crossing that busy street like that. Clearly her fault, but you did flee the scene of the crime."

"Yeah."

"Yeah. Major fuck-up, and Kurt says you were under the influence at the time."

"Not by much."

"A tiny bit and you'd be fucked beyond all recognition. But your test came clean. You're going to get the felony hit and run charge, a fine, some community service, a one year suspended sentence, five years probation."

"What's a suspended sentence?"

"You keep out of trouble for the five years, you don't have to worry. Get into any trouble, you'll do the year—which means you'll probably do four months. But you *don't* want to do any time."

"No."

"So," he said, "we go into court, you plead guilty to the hit and run, you sign a shitload of paperwork, and that's that."

"I can go home then?" I asked.

* * * * * * *

The process was easier than I'd thought. There were a lot of my fellow jailhouse mates standing in line; we were like pigs heading for the grinder. I was paying Waxman three grand for this?

I'd been a man on borrowed time. I knew I deserved this.

After the judge proclaimed my sentence, a man in the pews stood up and said, "That is all? He is not going behind bars?" He had a thick Eastern European accent. "He murders my sister and he doesn't have to pay for his crime?!?"

"Order!" the judge said.

"THIS IS AN OUTRAGE!"

"Mister," the judge said, "there will be no such outbursts in this court!"

I turned and looked at the man. He was tall and muscular, swarthy; wore a beard and glasses, and he was balding. He glared at me with pale blue eyes.

"I will have justice," he said to me, "and I will make you pay for my sister's murder!!!"

"Bailiff!" the judge cried. "Remove that individual from my courtroom!"

The man went without a fight, but kept staring at me.

Wonderful, I thought.

12.

It felt very nice to be back in my apartment. There were some messages on the answering machine. I didn't listen to a single one. I went to bed. I slept for twenty-four hours straight.

13.

Someone was knocking at my door. Through the peephole, the short redheaded woman in white shorts looked harmless. I opened the door.

She asked my name.

I said yes.

She handed me some folded papers and told me that I had been served. She walked away. I was confused.

The papers consisted of a summons to the Los Angeles Superior Court and a complaint for wrongful death and negligent infliction of emotional distress, filed by Pieter Dragamenchenko.

The woman's brother.

He was asking for two million dollars in damages.

Wonderful, I thought.

* * * * * * *

"I'm sorry this happened to you, Robert," Max Waxman said on the phone, "but civil litigation isn't my area of expertise. What I do is keep people out of the slammer. Your check cleared, by the way, and I thank you. I know a very good attorney who handles civil matters. In fact, she's very, *very* good. She'll do right by you. Would you like her number?"

"Sure."

"Her name's Lisa Dean. Tell you what, let me call her first. Then she'll call you, and she'll make that little problem of yours go away. Don't worry, Robert. Your life will get back to normal."

14.

Lisa Dean was an associate at the law firm of Fritz & Fitzgerald. She had a male secretary in a Brooks Brothers suit. I figured I was probably going to have to use my credit cards to pay for this legal counsel.

She was my age, something I wasn't expecting. I had to remind myself there were people my age running the business and entertainment world in this town. Knowing this didn't help my self-esteem.

I didn't expect such an attractive woman, either. Attractive isn't the word; beautiful or gorgeous wouldn't describe her. She was beyond sexy, *she was sex*. She was Ally McBeal on crack. I don't think I'd ever seen a shorter skirt in a business-ensemble. She didn't wear pantyhose, and her legs were southern California tanned and well-defined. The best casting director in all of Hollywood couldn't have done better. I'd just stepped into an erotic movie. Her dirty blonde hair was pulled back in a tail, accentuating her forehead and large brown eyes. Her hand was moist and warm and pulsating—when I shook it and we introduced ourselves. She looked me up and down, and took her time, and didn't hide this. She was a predator, she was letting me in on this from the start—hell, *she was a lawyer.*

"So," she said, walking towards her desk, her ass swaying, "you're getting sued."

I handed her the legal papers and sat down. I watched her carefully as she read the documents. Her thick red lips moved as she did so.

She asked, "Do you want to settle this?"

"I don't think I have the money," I said softly. "In fact, I know I don't have the money."

"I didn't ask you if you had the money, buster boy, I asked if you wanted to settle. We can offer this guy and his third-rate lawyer one dollar."

"I don't want to settle. I did nothing wrong. It wasn't my fault—the cops even said so."

"Exactly," she said. "This lawsuit is bullfuckingshit. They just want to see if they can get any money out of you. Maybe they think you're feeling guilty. *Are* you feeling guilty?" She lowered her voice and leaned forward.

"A little."

"A little is too much. You have nothing to feel guilty about."

"The woman is dead—"

"And it was *her* fault."

I nodded, and then I told her about the threat the woman's brother made in court.

"He was talking out of his ass," Lisa Dean said. "Tell you what." She stood, walked across her office, and sat down on the leather couch. I turned and looked at her. "I can move to have this dismissed. I happen to know the assigned judge *really* well. That's always an advantage in my line of work. When you get right down to it, it's all about people, and who you know."

I'd heard that one before.

"What do you think, Robert?"

"I think it's a good idea, Ms. Dean."

"Can I call you Bobby?"

"Sure."

"I like how that sounds—Bobby." She reached back and let her hair loose. The action was magical. She ran her hands through it. "And you can call me Lisa."

"Lisa," I said.

She opened her legs. The skirt was riding high and she wasn't wearing underwear. There wasn't a pubic hair on her. It looked so smooth. Her pussy lips opened up and I saw, without a doubt, that she was wet.

"Let's seal our deal, attorney-client," she said, and laughed. "Strictly confidential, if you know what I mean."

I couldn't move.

"What's the matter?" she asked. She reached down and touched herself. "Don't you want to fuck me, Bobby-boo?"

Yes I did, oh yes I did, and without thinking, I went to her. I pushed her back onto the couch and kissed her. I shoved my hand between her legs and felt how hot and wet she was. I unzipped my pants and gave her the fuck she wanted—I wanted—right then and there.

After, she stood and smoothed her skirt down. She walked back to her desk and sat.

She said, "I'll get a hearing date for the motion, you don't need to be there. It'll be an in-chambers thing. My secretary has the necessary paperwork ready for my retainer fee. You can pay by check or credit card. Any questions, Bobby?"

"Well," I said, "no."

"Good. I'll be in touch. Have a nice day."

15.

Lisa Dean called me three weeks later and told me that the judge had dismissed the lawsuit based on the grounds that there weren't sufficient facts to sustain the cause of action.

"It was tricky," she said softly, "but I always get my way."

I sighed. "Thank you."

"You can thank me by taking me out to dinner tonight," she said.

"Okay," I said.

16.

I met her at an Italian restaurant in Santa Monica. I had no idea I was being followed—one never does.

Lisa Dean was already there, sitting at the table, having a glass of white wine. Men in the restaurant were looking at her. She wore another very short skirt, black leather this time, with a white blouse and black leather jacket. Her hair was down and she'd gone heavy on the make-up and perfume.

I asked the waiter for a Long Island Iced Tea and sat across from my lawyer.

"Am I late?"

"You're on time," she said. "I'm always early." She leaned back. Her blouse was unbuttoned low. I caught a glimpse of one pink nipple. She wanted me to see it. She knew what she was doing. "This is my second glass of wine. Do you know how many times I've been hit on since I've been here?"

"I probably couldn't count."

"Not once. Oh, there are the eyes all right. But this is a civilized and refined establishment. If I was in a regular bar, I would have been accosted, hit on, proposed to, and maybe even raped a dozen times over. But not in a boring place like this. I hate boring places, don't you?"

"Why'd you pick this place then?"

"The steak and lobster are to die for."

The waiter came by with my drink.

Lisa Dean held up her wine glass. "A toast, to a man whose now out of trouble."

"I'll drink to that," I said.

The waiter was still there. "Shall I bring a menu?" He was trying to look down her blouse.

"I'll order for both of us," she said, and ordered two plates of the steak and lobster special.

I didn't tell her that I wasn't fond of lobster.

"So," she said, leaning back again.

"So," I said.

I felt her leg against mine.

"What will you do now?" she asked.

I didn't have a chance to answer. Pieter Dragamenchenko was in the restaurant. He'd followed me here, that was my first guess. He screamed my name, said that I murdered his sister and the United States was protecting a pig like me. He had a gun in his hand.

Lisa Dean leaped across the table like a hunted animal and grabbed me. Her nails scratched my face. She pulled me to the floor, under the table.

Bullets began to fly.

Several men became heroes in the restaurant—they wrestled the disgruntled Russian man down. He was big and it wasn't easy. Someone in a tux took the gun from him.

Lisa Dean pulled me up. She took my hand and said, "Let's get out of here."

"He just tried to kill me."

"He tried to kill *us*, kiddo. That's why we need to get the heck out of Dodge."

17.

Our hands clasped, she led me to her car, a silver Porsche. It was quite a car. My adrenaline was too pumped up to properly admire her set of wheels.

Lisa Dean was very excited by all this.

We got into her car, and we drove away very *very* fast. I could tell she liked to drive fast.

"You sure know how to show a girl a wild night," she said, like she was out of breath.

"Do you have to drive so crazy?"

"Does it bother you?"

"Yes."

She pouted. "Poor *baby*."

She was nuts, but I didn't know how nuts, until she made a strange suggestion.

18.

She pulled into a Burger King and we got some hamburgers. I didn't think I'd be hungry. The hamburger tasted good.

"Well, that some something," my lawyer said.

"What do you think will happen to him?"

"Attempted murder, he'll go away for a quite a while. I'm sure the police will want to talk to us. You, for sure. You were the target. Maybe I was a target, too. It's funny to think that."

"Should we go back?"

"Not just yet. There's something we need to do. There's something I need *you* to do for me. Call it a favor, for saving your life. Will you do me a favor, Bobby-boo?"

"Sure, I guess. What?"

"Let's go to my place," she said.

"Okay," I said.

* * * * * * *

She lived in Manhattan Beach and had a great view of the ocean. I felt depressed.

On her living room floor was a naked and gagged man in his fifties. He was thin and pale and had gray hair.

"Okay," I said, "what's going on?"

"Mr. Riker," Lisa Dean said, "meet Nelson Lake." She smiled at me. "I should say His Honor Judge Nelson Lake of the Los Angeles Superior Court."

"What?"

"How the hell do you think I got your lawsuit so easily dismissed? Like I said before, it's not what you know, it's who. Sometimes in the legal profession, it's who you *do.*"

I backed away. "This is getting too weird."

"It hasn't even *begun* to get weird." She was excited again, like she was being shot at. "I'm sure ol' Judge Lake here is wondering why we're back so early. See, Bobby, we were supposed to have dinner, a few drinks, maybe a walk, and I'd bring you here, and we'd get busy on the Judge. He thought he was going to spend a few more hours in the dark all tied up. Didn't you, Mr. Judgy-wudgy?"

She kicked him in the side.

He looked at her. His eyes were filled with rapture.

Lisa Dean turned to me. "Don't look so scared."

"I'm not."

"You *look* scared."

"Well," I said, "I'm not." I was.

"You said you'd do me a favor."

"What is it that you want me to do?" I asked.

"Hang on. Wait right there. I'll just be a minute or two. *Don't* you go anywhere."

She left.

I looked at the man on the floor. He tried to say something. I didn't want to know what he was trying to say.

I didn't know if this was a sex game or if he was here against his will.

I found that I didn't care.

Lisa Dean returned wearing nothing but knee-high leather boots. She looked wonderful naked, but at this point I didn't want anything to do with either the woman or her body.

She had an assortment of items—two whips, an enema bag, a crowbar and a cam-corder.

"What I want you to do," she said, "is be my cameraman."

"Your what?"

"You'll operate this camera," she said, "while I do some vile and horrible things to the judge."

"You have to be kidding me."

"No, I'm not."

"I don't want to do this."

"You owe me."

"This is nuts."

"No," she said, "it's kinky."

"What the fuck," I said, "I'll do it."

I tried not looking at her breasts or shaved pussy when she handed me the video camera.

19.

I left two hours later. I just walked out. I headed down to the beach. I hated the smell of the ocean. I waved down a passing cab and went home.

My car was still at the restaurant in Santa Monica.

I'd just spent two hours taping Lisa Dean doing some very perverted, smelly, and odd things to that judge. She had the whole ordeal on tape for prosperity, I guess. She said the tapes were better than porn, they were "avant-porn."

I never felt more dirty...

The night wasn't over; before I opened the door to my apartment, I felt a hand on my shoulder.

"Hey there, mon, don't jump," a voice from my past said.

I turned around. It was the Rastafarian guy from Las Vegas. He wore a lavender suit and it looked ridiculous on him.

"You remember me, mon?" he asked. "I saved your life."

"Yes."

"You owe me for that."

"Seems like I'm owing everyone for it," I said.

"Let's go inside and talk," he said.

"Do we have to?"

"I need your help on a job, mon."

20.

Inside my apartment, I asked, "How the hell did you find me? How do you know who I am? I never told you my name. I never told you a thing about me. It was such a bizarre encounter in Vegas I was starting to think it never happened."

"Your license plate, you idiot," he laughed. "I took down your numbers, I find out your name and address."

"Oh."

"My name is Gregory," he said. "I a hit man, mon."

"No kidding."

"I here in the City of the Angeles to do a job."

"And you need my help."

"That I do."

"I can't get involved in a fucking hit on someone," I said. I threw my hands up for a dramatic effect.

Gregory looked very serious. "You owe me your life, mon."

Under his jacket, I could see the gun he had in a shoulder-holster.

21.

We drove in his generic Ford rental car. I felt claustrophobic, sitting next to Gregory the Rastafarian hit man.

"This the plan, mon," he said. "My mark is inside a gay night club. My mark may recognize me—he know there is a price tag on his head. We've run into each other from time to time, y'know, and he knows what I do for a livin', y'know."

"No," I said, "I don't know."

"In a gay club, I'll stick out. He sees me, he makes a run for it, things get messy. We want this hit to go smooth, if y'know what I mean, my friend."

"No," I said, "I don't know what you mean."

"We go in as a couple."

"You and me?"

"Yah, mon."

"What, do I look gay?" I asked.

"Don't take nothin' personally," he said, laughing. "What do I know, what and who looks gay or not? We go in as a couple…"

"Great."

"You owe me."

"Yeah, yeah. I do this, we're even? I don't owe you nothing?"

"Even steven," he said.

22.

"Tell me something," I said. "Leon in Neon. Why did you kill him? What did he do?"

"One of his wives pay me to kill him, mon," Gregory said. "Ol' Leon was a bigamist."

"You knew him?"

"We crossed paths."

"Do you often 'cross paths' with the people you kill?"

"Not often," he said. "Y'see, one of his wives is my sister."

"I see."

"But she not the one who hired me. One of the other wives did the hirin'."

"I see."

"You don't mess around with the women like that. It always gets you in trouble."

I nodded.

23.

The club was in West Hollywood. I'd heard about the club. It was popular and had display lights in front. I could hear the music inside—thick on the bass, very danceable.

Gregory took my hand when we walked up to the entrance.

"Just don't kiss me," I said.

"You too ugly to kiss, mon."

He paid the twenty dollar cover charge, and we went in.

It was like any other club: dark, smoky, loud; the smell of sweat and anticipated sex glued to the brick walls.

There weren't as many patrons as I thought. But it was getting late. I hoped that Gregory's "mark" had gone home.

I wasn't that lucky. Gregory spotted him.

"There he is."

The mark was a man in his mid-thirties, well-dressed and good-looking in that L.A. gay sort of way, sitting at a table with two other men, just as well-dressed and good-looking.

Gregory nudged me. He'd told me what I was to do. I had no idea if it would work or what kind of assistance I'd be contributing to the proposed death of this man.

I did it, anyway.

The man's name was Ralphie. He looked up as I approached and he raised an eyebrow.

("You need to distract him so I can make my move," Gregory had told me.)

I smiled and said, *"Ralphie!"*

"Do I know you?" he asked, and smiled.

"Ralphie!" I said again. I sat at his table. The other two men stared at me, confused.

Ralphie was confused too. Was I a one-night stand he didn't recall? Was I good-looking enough to be someone he'd know? I had decent clothes on, at least—I'd put on my best for the dinner date with Lisa Dean.

"It's been a long time, Ralphie, a real long time," I said, wondering how my acting was.

"I'm afraid I don't know who you are," he said, amused.

"You don't remember me?"

"No."

"But Mr. Kenneth remembers you, Ralphie mon." Gregory's voice was loud.

Ralphie looked up and said, "Oh fuck."

I moved away from the table, fast.

Gregory had a gun with a silencer. He put three quick bullets into Ralphie's chest.

One of the men at the table went for a gun beneath his jacket. Gregory shot him once in the head.

The second man grabbed me by my jacket. He turned me around and punched me in the jaw. I tasted blood.

Gregory shot him twice.

I spat out a tooth.

"Let's go," Gregory said.

No one tried to stop us.

24.

I was rubbing my bloody gums, lamenting about my lost tooth. My jaw was throbbing. Gregory was driving the rental car at a legal speed. He was a man who never worried about anything.

"You did good," he said.

"It's over?" I said.

"Oh yes, your night is over."

"This has been the longest night of my life."

When he dropped me off at my apartment building, he said, "Next time, we do lunch. I buy you a drink or somethin', mon."

"Don't take this personally," I said, "but I'd rather never see you again."

He laughed. "I understand, mon."

25.

The night still wasn't over. There was someone waiting for me in my apartment. He was a big man, and he was sitting on my couch, holding a spiral-bound notebook and drinking from a fifth of Gordon's vodka.

"Don't be alarmed," he said.

"I'm not," I said. "How did you get in?"

"Your back window was unlocked."

"You're here to kill me," I said. "So just do it. I'm ready. Kill me. Maybe I deserve it."

Pieter Dragamenchenko stood up. He was drunk, his eyes were red. It looked like he'd been crying.

"Yes, I wanted to kill you," he said in his slurred accent. "I tried killing you and that bitch lawyer tonight…"

"Yeah," I said. I didn't know what to do here.

"I got away. They called the police but I got away. I went home. I knew the police would come for me there. My mother was waiting up for me. My sister and my mother, we all lived in the same small apartment, coming here to America."

I knew this; Lisa Dean had told me.

"My dear mother, she finds this." The big Russian tossed the notebook my way. I quickly caught it. "Go ahead, you look."

I opened the notebook, waiting for Dragamenchenko to pull out a gun or knife and end my short unhappy life.

The notebook was filled with a lot of small handwriting, all in the Russian alphabet.

"I don't know how to read this," I said.

He was crying now.

"She was dying," he said. "You didn't kill her. *She killed herself!*"

It took a while; the Russian explained to me that his mother had gone through her departed child's belongings and found the notebook, a diary. In it, she wrote about coming to the United States, getting a job in Los Angeles, and then seeing a doctor. She wasn't feeling well. She was told she had leukemia, and the disease would kill her in a year or two. She couldn't face telling her family, or having to get treatments with enormous hospital bills. She was very depressed, but put on a face for her family: all was well and she was happy. She knew she had to end her life, and mapped out her plan in the diary: she would step into the busy intersection at Wilshire and Santa Monica. She'd seen many accidents there before. She knew it was a cowardly way to go, but she was getting sicker and there was no other way.

It wasn't my fault.

All this guilt, everything, and it wasn't my fault.

That bitch.

"Oh shit," I said.

The Russian still had tears in his eyes. "I am sorry for trying to hurt you."

* * * * * * *

I helped Pieter finish the Gordon's. I had a bottle of Skyy and we drank that too. The alcohol hurt my bleeding gums, but the pain soon faded to numbness.

The irony didn't escape me. If the notebook had been found sooner, many of the things that happened to me would not have happened.

If I hadn't gone to Vegas...

If I hadn't gone to Adrian's party...

If I'd left the party two minutes later, or earlier...

I told Pieter these things, and he nodded, and we drank.

I looked out a window and almost laughed. "This has been the most insane night of my life," I said.

"The sun is almost up," said the Russian.

"It's nice," I said, "daylight."

"Yes," he said, "yes, it is."

SEXY STRUMPET

Looked like it was going to rain up there, the way the clouds were gathering. Downtown was packed with all sorts of Saturday night party people. I was wearing a long leather trench; my long hair was messy and I knew I had dark circles under my eyes. I went to one of the topless bars. The doorman checked my ID, gave me a glance, said, "Something eating you, buddy?"

"What?"

"Seem a little nervous there. Never been to a titty and pussy club?"

Grinned. "Well, I just got out of the pen."

"Enjoy," he said.

There were two stages, two girls; the girls changed every third song. When they didn't dance, they served drinks. I ordered a pitcher of beer but I didn't drink.

I watched the backroom.

I saw a fat man in a good suit come out, count some bills from the register and then go back in. Got up and followed him.

Didn't knock on the office door that had a little sign:

PRIVATE

Underneath the trench, I retrieved the sawed-off pump-action I'd been toting, hiding, waiting—yes—nervously to use, for this very moment.

Barged in.

All three of them were fat and their shirts were dirty, greasy from fallen food; but their suits were real nice and they had shit-eating grins as they counted the money in front of them.

"Hey," one of them started to say, "you're—"

Then he saw the sawed-off.

Another one went for the revolver tucked in his stretched waistline.

"Tsk, tsk," I went, and waved the sawed-off.

The third went for the phone.

"Nope," I said.

"Hey, asshole," the fat fuck who got the money from the register said, "what the hell do you want, huh?"

"Ah, the Martoni brothers," I said. "Best pizza this side of town. Best sleazy stripper joint, too."

"Yeah, that's us," said one of the brothers. "Who are you?"

"A dancer used to work here."

"Lots of dancers work here. They comes and go."

"Her name was Rhonda Littlefield."

Silence.

"You know what I'm talking about. She was murdered three months ago."

One of them said, "Yeah, poor Rhonda. Sexy little strumpet, she was."

Another said, "What about her?"

A third said, "We had nothing to do with that."

I said, "She was my sister."

"She hung around the wrong kind of people, you know?" I was told. "Her own fault."

The door behind me opened. I opened started shooting. One of the dancers came in—fake platinum blonde with fake tits, wearing a bra and a g-string. She started to say something and stopped when she saw me and the sawed-off.

"Get in," I said and grabbed her thin arm.

"Is this a hold-up?" she said, chewing bubble gum.

I pushed her toward the Martoni brothers and said, "Just stay put and keep quiet."

"You want money, is that it?" one of the brothers asked me. "Here it is, pal, take it."

"What I want," I said, "is to know which one of you fat fucks killed my sister."

Silence.

"Hey, you knew Rhonda L., right?" one of them asked the platinum blonde.

She had to think about it. "Rhonda? Yeah, sure. We hung out once or twice."

"Well, this is her brother, that's what he says. You tell him how she was. Picking up strange men from this place all the time. Never safe. Drugs. She just got with one of the weirdoes, cut her up and stuff. We had nothing to do—you tell him, Lynn, you tell he brother what kind of nasty bitch his sister was."

The platinum blonde was shaking now. She looked at the sawed-off, then me, said, "Rhonda L. was kind of wild, you know."

"I know one of you did it," I said. "All I want—which one? Which one, or I blow all three of you whales away."

One of them said, "Hey, boy, where do you get such an idea it was one of us? We're not like that."

With my free hand, I took out a small diary from the trench pocket. "Chronicles of a life, penned by Rhonda Littlefield," I said. "Talks all about how she goes to work at one of the Martoni Brothers Pizza Houses. Then she gets talked into working here: wiggling tits and ass, flashing her cunt and serving drinks. Tells all about how she gets coaxed into bed by one of the Martoni brothers—no name, just one of them. 'They're all fat and disgusting,' she writes. But she goes to bed with this fat fucker because he knows about her secret— a little habit-now-problem with cocaine. So he gets her hooked on more so she'll sleep with him. Then, one day, she winds up dead in a cheap motel room. Now, I either find out which one of you killed her, or you all die."

Silence.

Two of them turned and looked at the third brother.

The third one said, "Okay, I gave her blow and she...was friendly. But I didn't kill her, pal. She liked to play rough, with me, with anyone. I didn't kill her."

I shot his head off.

It was messy.

The two remaining brothers had their dead brother's blood, bone and brain all over them.

The platinum blonde held a hand over her mouth.

Then I took out the other two the same way.

The blonde and I stared at each other.

The music in the club was loud; no one heard the shot-gun fire.

"Are you going to kill me too?" she asked very softly.

"You never saw my face," I said. "You never saw me at all."

"Never! Never! I don't know what you look like, I didn't even know there was someone in here with—"

"That's good."

"Oh man what a mess," she said. "Can I scream now? I really need to."

"When I'm gone."

"How will I—"

"Three minutes," I said, and started to go.

"Hey, you really Rhonda L.'s brother?"

I tossed her the diary and she caught it nervously. "Keep it. Write in it."

Her mouth opened and the bubble gum fell out when she saw that all the pages were blank.

"How did," she started to say.

But I left.

SWAMP HARLOT

Me: serial killer, an all-time fan of Phyllis Diller; master of the crossing-the-state-line slaughter, making the headlines after killing the Alabama preacherman's daughter; at the tender age of eighteen, I offed my momma and the feds wanted me for that, just that, they hadn't yet linked me to the chop-chop-chops I'd done from East to South and West and then back, West to South now heading East. I was in Baton Rouge, Louisiana; I didn't know these parts too well but it was in Baton Rouge, Louisiana that I found kill Number Twenty-Six, and my future wife. Number Twenty-Six was twenty-one or two with a belle name like Sally-Lou or Soozie Bleu, sweet and pretty, saw her in a blues bar and she was drunk, told me, "cuz my asshole beau that I thought was a beau isn't my beau no mo' cuz he's off fuckin' some other cunt," and seeing her in that tight, tight blue dress and those black pumps on small feet and those bare white legs, on that barstool, bombed, eyes half-closed, swaying this-away and that-away to the saxman and the bass and piano, I knew she had to be Number Twenty-Six, so I slid over there, beer in hand, asking if I could get her another drink; she looked at me and said, "Sure, you cute funny-talkin' thin'." I took her back to my cheap motel room, which was perfect, no one would remember me (I signed in with an alias as always). Stripped her naked, she gave me head, I fucked her like I fucked them all, the bitches, and I slapped her some, hard, slapped her unconscious, took the blades and razors from the trusty black satchel I carry, and proceeded to slice'n'dice. She came to as I was making her wholeness into moreness, started to scream; I slit her throat and that was the end of that. I played in all the blood and gore like a ba-by pig in mud. I gathered all her parts into the available sheets and blankets, bundled them good and tight, took them out to my car in the middle of the night, stuck it all in the trunk, got the rest of my stuff and got the hell out of there ---

Somewhere out there on the outskirts of Baton Rouge, I came across the swampy marsh—or marshy swamp.

Parked, got the southern gal's bundled parts, and gave them the heave-ho into the water.

I heard a sound—a moan, a movement; not far from me, a few yards.

It was a girl. She was lying on the ground; dirty jeans, torn blouse, a gash on forehead. I went to her, looked at her; she was staring up at me, eyes blank, mouth open. I thought I was the Lucky Dog of this night—I had me Number Twenty-Seven. I glanced around, making sure there wasn't someone in the lurks with her, a set-up—but no, I thought, look at her, whoever she'd been with did this to her, banged her up, left her here. Looking closer, she grinned, a grin I would later know all too well—it was then I realized she would *not* be kill Number Twenty-Seven.

She sat up, seemed confused. She touched her blouse, jeans. "What...is this?" Her voice was opaque as this southern night.

"What happened?" I knelt by her. "Are you okay?"

S he pulled at the fabric of the blouse, said, "What is this on my body?"

I laughed.

"Who are you?"

I told her my name, my real name, which surprised me.

I held out my hand, to help her up. She just looked at it.

I stood. "Not the friendly type?"

She tried to stand, nearly fell. I caught her. She said, "My head is dizzy."

"How did you get out here?" Our faces were close—made me nervous.

"I...do not know," she said, distraught.

"Did you come out here alone?"

"Always alone," she said, a whisper. I thought she was going to faint. I asked her name. She didn't know: "I don't have a name," she said; she didn't have a southern accent.

I said, "You're not from these parts."

"I am," she replied. "I'm from there," she pointed to the swamp. Asked if she needed a ride. "I have to get going."

"Ride?"

"My car is—"

"Yes," she said.

That's how I met my wife.

* * * * * * *

Happened fast—we got married a few weeks later. Kept wondering why I didn't want to kill her. There was something she possessed—or did not possess—from other women; she didn't bring out the rage within, the hate and the fear, the subsequent desire to see them hurt and bleed, to see their bodies torn apart by my hands and instruments. She asked so many questions, life and cities and towns and the world. I knew I'd never hurt her. I'd love her, I was already in love. Whoever, however, she was beaten and left in the night—the violation she endured but didn't recall—the end result was amnesia. She didn't know her name, past, where she was born and grew up, or what she'd done yesterday. She kept telling me she came from the swamp. She wasn't crazy, and she could be taught how to function in the world again. For now, I was her world; I took pleasure in this—*me me me*. I asked if she wanted to come to New York. "New York?" she said. Told her it was a big city where we'd have lots of fun and lots to see. She said, "Yes, yes, I want to go," and so we did. We stayed in a motel room; we slept in the same bed but didn't have sex. I wanted to. Something pure stopped me. She pranced around our room naked like she didn't know what naked was; she didn't understand why she had to wear clothes when we went outside. She needed new clothes; I bought them for her. She needed a name; I called her "Amnesia." I was running out of cash, fast. We needed a real place to live. I went out one night and picked-up a fifty-something woman in a Park Avenue bar. She looked like money. She took me to her Park Avenue apartment, told me hubby-wubby was on a business trip in Europe. "Probably balling his twenty-year-old secretary," she slurred, drank more, told me she wanted to ball. Usually I do, only to make it worse, or better, but tonight I was thinking of Amnesia. My love. I hit the woman on the back of the head with my fist. Opened satchel, placed on gloves, checked the apartment. In the study—her hubby-wubby's no doubt—I found a wall safe. Easy to get into. Thirty-eight grand plus some jewelry—necklaces and rings made of diamonds and things. The woman was starting to come to; I hit her again. Chopped her into seven, eight pieces. I hoped I didn't smell like death—after all these years, it's hard to tell. I didn't want my love to smell this.

I was quiet when returning to our room. The TV was on—snow—she was asleep. She opened her eyes, said she missed me. "Look what I have for you," and I held up a pearl necklace. She smiled. I put it on her. She didn't ask where it'd come from, or the rest of the jewelry and cash. She didn't know about the world.

Next day, we rented an apartment in Chelsea. It was nice, cozy. I knew that if we were to settle down, I would have to become a citizen, get a job,. I couldn't go on forever, wandering the nation chop-chop-chopping my merry way along. I thought: *This is it.* I was happy. One night, Amnesia and I were watching my heroine, Phyllis Diller, on the boob, a re-run, the woman was in best form, so funny, I was crying I was laughing so much—Amnesia laughing along although she didn't understand the humor, she just wanted to laugh with me. My love reached out and we kissed. I felt it, I knew it, I said, "Let's get married; let's be man and wife." She said yes yes. I said I finally wanted to, now, make love to her. She didn't know what that was. I asked, "You've never had sex?" She didn't know. I took her to bed. We undressed. She was curious, she giggled. After I did a few things with finger and mouth, she sighed and said, "Why haven't we ever done this before?" When I entered her, she throbbed, came, cried out, "We have to do this all the time!"

* * * * * * *

I got a job selling men's suits. I liked the work and I was making decent commission. Amnesia didn't like that I was out for eight hours a day; all she wanted to do was screw like some southern Lou-Lou. She began to frequent the library on Forty-Second Street, reading anything and everything. I was, at first, afraid she'd get her memory back. I stopped worrying after a while—she loved me, this was true, this I knew: if she did recall, she could never deny her feelings, the best of all. Besides, she was my legal wife now. On the marriage certificate she was listed as Amelia Marsh, but I still called her Amnesia. After several months and a few hundred books, she told me she didn't want to be known by that name. "Call me Amelia," she declared.

I had quit the chop-chop-chops. Two years since that last one. The opportunities didn't come and the need to drive and hide wasn't outside. Eventually, however, it did come—I knew it wouldn't be gone forever. There had to be a Number Twenty-Eight. Another middle aged woman with cash bought some suits from me, said they were for her brother; she asked me to lunch. "I like being blunt, no playing around," she said, "and I like the way you look." Told her I was married. "So am I," she said, "and I'll pay you for your time if you want." I felt it then, just a bit: the hate, THE AVERSION , *the wave*. I thought this might be a good break from the pleonastic existence (as Amelia referred to it) I was leading as suits salesman. She said she had a hotel room, showed me the key. I followed her there. I used my belt to strangle her. I called room service, ordered a roast, asked for a nice big carving knife, told them to leave it by the door. I placed a twenty outside. Couldn't afford to be seen by anyone. I waited a bit, brought the cart in. The roast smelled good. I took the long, sharp knife and went to work on the woman. I made sure I cleaned my prints from anything I might've touched. I was excited—*this was just like old times.* What had I missed?! Still, there was that guilt. Coming home, I hugged and kissed my wife and wondered how I could've done this to her. Why can't I be a regular man with a life, wife, home, maybe kids? I mentioned children to her. "Maybe later," she said, "right now I want to enroll in college."

* * * * * * *

She went to CCNY in Brooklyn. At least she had something to do now. I continued to work while she, over the next three years, worked on a degree in sociology. During that time, I killed six other women. They came along and I couldn't help myself. I was the manager of the suit store now. I tried not to hire women because the urge might arise and I'd do something—well, I needed strangers. I found them in bars—office workers, relaxing with a drink, maybe a fuck. It was that sixth one—Number Thirty-Four—that brought it all to an end. She was an assistant editor at some pulp paperback publishing house. We went to her flat, not far from my place. "My roommate will be gone all week," she giggled, kissed me. We went to the waterbed, I had her, she said be rough, so I was rough, slammed her forehead into the wall, sodomized her, choked her, body red and blue. I opened my trusty satchel and whistled as I worked. This job was messy—blood all over my clothes. I ran home, knowing Amelia would be late from school. I tried washing the blood from my clothes in the bath tub. Amelia came up behind me and said, "You should just burn those, you know. Best way: no evidence."

I jumped, I screamed. I said, "Amelia!—I—I was mugged—mugged while coming home and they hit me and I got bl—"

"Don't try to lie," she said, calmly. "That blood's from your latest kill. Thirty-two now? Or more? Do you still keep count?"

I was silent.

She smiled. "I've known all along, since the first night we met. You're a serial killer, have been since you were a kid. I've known about almost every one of them, my dear. I don't care. It's in your nature, you do what you have to do. You're my husband and I love you and that's why I'm telling you we should just *burn* those clothes."

I freaked—thought she was messing with my head. She was humoring me; I was a psycho and she wanted to calm me down so she could call the cops. *My own wife was going to turn me in!* I howled, slammed my fist into the side of her head. Her eyes rolled. I hit her again. She fell to the floor. I kept pounding until her face was a fleshy pulp. I opened the trusty satchel and did a number, the cleanest and best of them all: chop-chop-chopping her into a dozen parts. I bundled her parts, crying the whole time. I was alone now, I didn't have any love in this world. Two a.m. I drove her parts to the Brooklyn Bridge. There was no one out. I tossed the bundles over. I cried the whole way home. *Alone*: I was going to have to deal with it.

* * * * * * *

She came back early in the morning.

I couldn't sleep. I was drinking a beer.

She walked in, dressed in the torn and bloodied dress she was wearing when it wasn't so torn and bloody. Her hair was wet. She grinned, leaning against the closed door. "It was a long walk back," she explained. "Had to go certain ways so no one would see me."

I took it rather placid. "But I killed you."

"No," she said, "you can't do that to me."

"I chop-chop—"

"I merely regenerated. It's simple."

I looked at my beer.

"Honey?"

I looked up.

"I guess now is a good time to tell you," she said.

"Yeah, why don't you?"

"Did you ever take a basic biology class in high school?"

I frowned. "What—"

"Do you remember studying about a flatworm species called a planarian?"

I drank my beer. "What the hell are you talking about, Amelia?"

"A planarian," she said, "can regenerate itself if cut into twos, fours, sometimes even sixes. If you teach one to go through a maze to get food, then you cut it up, the other pieces will also know how to go through the maze." She sighed, leaning further into the door. "It would be too difficult to explain to you what I am, where I come from, and how I came to be. But let's just say that I'm like a planarian. You see, they live in water, like swamps and creeks. Like the swamp you found me, where I once dwelled. You remember, love?"

"Louisiana," I said.

"My kind have lived in swamps like that for centuries. Never coming out. That particular swamp seemed to be a favorite dumping site for murdered victims. You weren't the first to hide a body in it. We fed off the flesh of those dead. We ingested your kind and learned about you. Came to a point where some of us wanted to be like you—big and masters of the world. I did, and I was the first to go. I took the from of one of the bodies, took it the night you came along. I crawled out and you found me. This was why I didn't understand clothes—I somehow also regenerated the clothes. Took me a while to adjust to many things. But I was persistent to be human, and finally I am. We are."

I started to laugh.

"What's so funny?"

"You say you can 'regenerate' like those worms—so what about all your other parts? I cut you into a doz—"

"That's the problem," she said, opening the door. She waved a hand. Eleven naked Amelias waltzed in, all grinning that grin I knew well, saying hello to me, some of them coming over and giving me a kiss.

"You shouldn't have chopped me into so many pieces," she—one of them—said.

"I'm not mad at you," another said, "you just over-reacted, and we *are* still married."

"And we are still in love," said another.

"At least you'll never be alone," three Amelias said in chorus.

TROUBLESOME TROLLOP

The first time I went to the bi-weekly evening gatherings of New York's most prominent playwrights, I was twenty-two, frightened, and intimidated. It was the Spring of 1909, and I remember the weather being unusually warm; or perhaps all the sweating I was doing under my old wool suit was due to nervousness. My first play had opened at a small theater to much critical (and little financial) success, thus I was invited to join the round-table of the city's renown masters of stagecraft. There was a little over a dozen of them at the mid-city townhouse where the gathering took place, all sitting around on deep sofas and plush chairs and drinking various liquids, ranging from wine to scotch and bourbon to tea. All but one were men; most in their late thirties to early forties, and the one woman among us was in her fifties. It caused me little comfort to know they all had been my age, or younger, when their first plays were mounted. However, to this day, most of them have faded into obscurity; for all their pomposity, they were doomed to a future of being neither in print nor on stage. There was one man there whose name you might recognize, though: Eugene O'Neill. I never got to know Mr. O'Neill well, much to my later disappointment and regret.

My story here is about Willard Reed, and *his* story he told that first time I went to the gathering. Did I mention they called themselves the Playwrights Chamber? That's who they were.

I wasn't sure what these people talked about. The art of writing theater, yes, that was expected; or maybe they would complain about certain producers, directors, and actors; or maybe the talk would not be of art, but of political ideals such as socialism and communism, heavy aspects in those mutable days in American history.

After I was introduced to everyone, someone said, "Last time, Willard promised to tell us his yarn of being a detective and how he solved a murder."

"Well," Willard Reed said, sipping at his bourbon, "it is a story of how I played an *amateur* detective. Unfortunately, I didn't solve the murder."

"Still," someone else from the group said, "it sounds like a fascinating tale."

Willard Reed smiled. He was a tall man, thick in the middle, wearing a black suit and tie. He held a cane in his hand. He was in his late forties, maybe early fifties, hard to tell. I'd seen several of his plays over the years. I found them to be rather lengthy and opprobrious, but he always had sad, tragic endings that touched me in the darkest spot of my heart. He cleared his throat. "This happened three months ago. You're all familiar with the Fritz Shakespeare Ensemble, I'm sure." Nods and mumbled yeses came from most of the people. I nodded; I'd heard of them, had even seen one of their productions of *The Tempest*. "A young and dynamic troupe that takes certain risks with the sacred William's words. I was most impressed with what they did with *Hamlet*. Three months ago, however, I was at the opening night soirée of their run of *Twelfth Night*. It was the usual after-glow gathering of a troupe having just completed hard work on a long and challenging project, and they were letting loose, with much booze, as is expected wherever actors—or even playwrights—are found," a few low chuckles, "and a bottle of Absinthe and even a small tray with snuff. I was keeping a low-profile, only a few people there knew who I was, and I didn't feel like making advertisements as to my status in the theater community."

"How unusual!" someone commented.

Others laughed in afterthought.

Reed seemed to find this amusing. He grinned, and reached to the table in front of him, where the bottle of bourbon was placed. He poured himself two fingers of the fine, light brown liquid. Myself, I was drinking white wine. I can't stomach hard alcohol, although I like the taste of good bourbon with bitters. I was licking my lips in anticipation, on two different levels.

The man crossed his legs and went on. "Being an astute observer, I noticed a minor drama taking place between three of the members of the company. A woman, and two men, as such dramas are bound by cliché. One of the men I knew—he is the artistic director of the group; he was, in fact, the person who had invited me to this after-show gathering. He was also an actor, but wasn't in the present production, the duties of running the company, as he had told me in a previous conversation, taking up more and more of his time, so that he found himself on stage less and less. His name was, is, Daniel Davis. He was having, what appeared to be, an emotional conversation with the young woman who had directed *Twelfth Night*. She was no more than thirty, with a round pretty face and large eyes, dark hair, thin build. Her name was Carla Black. I must put emphasis on the past tense 'was', as she would, the next morning, be found murdered in an alley."

There were some gasps from the group, but I felt they were feigning this shock to add tension to the suspense Willard Reed was building. I, for one, may have been disinterested at first, but he now had my rapt attention, because I recalled hearing about the murder of one of the members of The Fritz Shakespeare Ensemble—Carla Black, a young and promising director.

"But back to the party," Reed said, sipping his bourbon with relish. "On first glance, while I could not hear what they were saying, huddled in a corner of the room, I might believe they were having a heated conversation about the opening night performance; about art, about ticket sales, anything quite innocent. But I knew innocence was not a factor as I took note of another man also watching them. This man had a part in the present show, and he was good, a somewhat overweight but passionate actor I had seen in other productions from this troupe, and at other theaters as well. His name was, and is, Bertrand Barkley.

"You know how you can feel hate from someone if they are looking at you and directing that hate toward you? You can feel the same when witnessing a person directing hate at another. And Mr. Barkley was commanding his hate towards Mr. Davis and Ms.

Black. He had a mug of beer in hand, and he was watching them, albeit afar, quite closely. Ms. Black glanced away from Davis, and she saw Barkley looking at her. Then Ms. Black started to go, to move away from Mr. Davis. Davis grabbed her arm, and she shrugged him away. I overheard her say: 'No, Daniel, no, it's over and it's never going to happen again.'

"There was another person who was also watching this incident—a young blonde girl of twenty, an actress who had a bit part in the show. I wasn't aware she was part of this, and he would prove herself to be a rather troublesome trollop, but I'm getting ahead of myself.

"Anyway," Reed continued, uncrossing his legs, "Ms. Black started to make her way to the middle of the room, perhaps to refresh her drink, when Mr. Barkley made his move to intercept her. He took her by the arm, and she didn't appear to be pleased by this. I was close enough to catch some of their conversation. Basically, Mr. Barkley wanted to know what she was talking to Mr. Davis about. She told him what it was none of his business but he insisted that it was. I heard Mr. Barkley say: 'You told me that it was over between you and him.'

"'It is,' Ms. Black said, *'it is.'*

"'Well, it doesn't seem like it is to me,' Barkley said.

"I noticed that, across the room, Mr. Davis was now watching these two conversing, and he had hate in his eyes as well.

"'It doesn't even matter,' Ms. Black said to Barkley.

"Mr. Barkley's reply was: 'Well, it matters a hell of a lot to me!'

"With this, Ms. Black stormed away, to another room, or perhaps outside. Mr. Barkley remained where he was, and he looked at Mr. Davis. Needless to say, the air between them, and the looks they gave one another, were far from friendly—for two men who worked in the same company.

"At this point, the young blonde actress appeared at my side, with a curious expression on her face. She was a small, bird-like creature, beautiful like an angelic child, I'd say. She was drinking Pernod, I could smell it from the glass in her hand. 'Quite a show, wouldn't you say?' she asked. She had a British accent."

"A British accent!" the only woman in the group said, with a thick British accent.

"Indeed," Willard Reed replied. "I asked about this. She said she was born in Herts, studied acting in London, and came to America. Her name was, and is, Cassandra Payne. This information was revealed a bit later in our conversation. The meat, we will say, of our rendezvous, was what both she and I had been watching. I had seen her observing the little drama just as she had taken note of my own observation. She knew who I was, much to my surprise. She even said she had auditioned for one of my plays. 'You were sitting there when I auditioned,' she told me.

"'I'm sorry I don't remember you,' I said, 'but when I go to auditions for my work, I see many—'

"And she cut me off, gently, touching my hand, saying, 'It's all right, I understand. You see many faces...'

"'I'm sure you gave a great audition,' I said. I felt foolish saying such. I wasn't at all sincere.

"Young Cassandra Payne didn't seem to register what I stated. She was preoccupied with the recent conflict we were both witness to. This is when I learned that Ms. Black was formally Mrs. Barkley. In fact, the divorce was still clogging through the court system and not finalized, and Ms. Black had never officially taken Barkley's last name, being the liberated sort of woman we meet more and more these days. Or so I was to understand by hearsay information.

"Ms. Payne gave me a quick synopsis of the history behind what had just transpired. Mr. Barkley was far from the man of fidelity, having been married to Carla Black for three years. He was known to have had a number of liaisons with actresses who came and went from the troupe. At first, he was able to keep his extramarital trysts secret, but soon Ms. Black found out, as such things always come apparent, and she wanted a divorce. Mr. Barkley agreed, and confessed he didn't love her anyway. But when Barkley learned that Ms. Black was having relations with Mr. Davis, he became infuriated. One would wonder why, but apparently there was artistic and aesthetic rivalry between Barkley and Davis to begin with. Also, Barkley had won the favor of some young women that Davis had set his eyes on, so they were on a high competitive level."

"Two cocks in a hen house," Eugene O'Neill said.

"Two bulls in a field of cows," added someone else.

"Indeed," Reed said. "Ms. Payne told me that the troupe was on the verge of falling apart because of this terrible threesome—the artistic director, the main stage director, and the main actor. Not to mention they were also the founders of the company! A bad stew brewing!

"Ms. Payne shook her head as she relayed this information. She looked very sad. I wanted to hug her, really I did. There was genuine pain in her eyes. I understood how such interpersonal conflicts could destroy a theater group. 'I understand how they both love her,' she told me. 'She's beautiful, she has charisma, she is a great director. She draws people to her, and they fall in love with her. But I'm afraid Daniel and Bertrand may kill each other over her.'

"'These things have a way of always working out,' I said, and again I felt foolish, for being a playwright, a scribe of human drama, these intricacies of human love—well, I must to admit to a certain amount of innocence and ignorance."

"What about her murder?" someone next to me asked, a man close to my age who seemed quite enthralled by the story, and drinking scotch.

"That is next," Willard Reed replied. He poured himself more bourbon. I looked at my wine glass: half-full. "The next day, when I read in the papers that Carla Black, theater director, was found with her stomach ripped open by a knife in an alley not but ten blocks from where the after-show party had taken place, my blood went cold. The paper said there were no suspects. Naturally, as I'm sure this is going through the rest of your minds, I deducted otherwise.

"I bathed and dressed and immediately went to the local police station, and inquired about the detective handling the murder case of Carla Black. I was introduced to Nick Henderson, a well-dressed, well-groomed man in his thirties, who was assigned the case. I told him who I was, and my interest in the murder. He assured me that there were no suspects yet, that it could very well have been a random slaying. She was walking home, she was accosted, she may have been raped, they hadn't checked the body yet. 'This is no Jack the Ripper case,' I told him, 'because I have two solid suspects for you.'

"He told me that he had talked to everyone in the Fritz Shakespeare Ensemble, but no one had seen her leave the party, alone or otherwise. I told him what I had seen, the arguments, and what I knew about the romantic love triangle. 'This could very well be a case of crime of passion!' I said.

"Henderson considered this, nodding his head, and agreed. However, he had already talked to both Davis and Barkley.

"'How did they take the news?' I asked.

"'They were both in shock,' he said.

"'They are both actors,' I informed him, 'and very *good* actors.'

"'Perhaps,' he said, 'I should talk to them again.'

"'But they're waiting for that,' I said, 'whichever one is the killer. The guilty party has prepared a story. But I have an idea.' This is where I fancied myself the detective. Of course, I have been reading, for years, the mysteries composed by Sir Arthur Canon Doyle, concerning the adventures of Sherlock Holmes and Dr. Watson. I don't know who I was seeing myself as—Mr. Holmes or Dr. Watson, but they were both my inspiration. So this is what I proposed to Detective Henderson:

"'Sir,' I said, 'whichever is the guilty party, they are presently waiting for you to confront them. We need to catch the culprit by surprise.' I outlined to the Detective my idea, and he agreed to it.

"I sent by bicycle messenger, early the next day, separate messages to both Mr. Davis and Mr. Barkley. I professed my deep regret for their loss of a company member, and my hope that the criminal responsible would be caught, charged, and convicted; then I offered an ideal situation: that I knew a man of wealth who was interested in underwriting a full season of their projects. Naturally, both men messengered me back, that afternoon, that they were interested in meeting with this possible arts philanthropist. Because of the animosity between the two, I assumed, correctly, there was a power struggle, and that garnering a rich benefactor would give either of them power over the other. Thus, I knew they would not tell one another of my correspondence.

"I had enough time to send a late messenger to both to come to my residence in the morning to meet the man with money—I told Barkley to arrive at ten, and Davis to arrive at ten-thirty.

"Detective Henderson was at my residence at nine o'clock. We went over and over my plan. I assured him this would work. Of course, I was feeling quite proud of myself, like a Sherlock Holmes, trapping the killer in an intellectual web.

"Barkley was at my door at nine-forty-five. I had a feeling he would be early, because he was my main suspect. He had a stronger motive—to kill, after all, his ex-wife, who was sleeping with a man who is his rival.

"I had tea and croissants to offer. I told him that the possible benefactor had not yet arrived. Detective Henderson, however, was situated in the closet, listening and waiting. At ten sharp, my bell rang. I answered the door, and allowed Mr. Daniel Davis into my home, and took him to the room where Mr. Barkley waited in a chair, and the police officer waited in a closet.

"Needless to say—"

"Needless to say," someone interrupted, "neither man was prepared for such a deception!"

"A deception, indeed," Reed said. "The ploy of the master detective! Or so I was fooling myself. Both men faced each other like two lions in a cage."

"Cocks," the British woman said.

"Cocks then. I knew I had to intervene quickly. I told them I had brought them both here because I knew that one of them was the murderer of Carla Black. I told them I had witnessed the scene at the party, and I knew, somewhat. the history between the three. At this point, much to my disappointment, Detective Henderson made his way out of the closet, and he was holding a Remington revolver in his hand. 'I too know the history between the three of you,' he said, 'and it is my belief that one of you killed her with a knife.'

"Both men broke down, simultaneously. They said Carla Black's death was the most devastating thing either had ever experienced, and they both stated they were not the culprit of her demise. And to my own shock, neither blamed the other.

"Together, they illustrated the history of this love triangle: how Barkley had, in fact, went to the beds of young actresses who joined the company, and Davis had done the same, and a rivalry of female conquests began between the two. Thus, when Barkley learned that his ex-wife, or soon-to-be-ex-wife, was sleeping with Davis, he became extremely jealous, and quite insecure.

"We were told that the affair between Davis and Ms. Black was brief; they had, in fact, only had two amorous encounters, and Ms. Black felt this was a bad idea, for the sake of the troupe, and that she really had no feelings for Davis. The sexual entanglings were, as she had told both men, 'a mistake in judgment.'

"Despite this, in my mind, as well as the detective's, they were still likely suspects. However, both men had alibis for the night. They had both left the party in the company of actresses. *In fact,* Mr. Barkley took Cassandra Payne to his home, the very girl whom had led me on this path. 'I drank a lot that night, I was very drunk,' Barkley said, 'but when I woke up, Cassy Payne was in my bed. This was no surprise, because she had been in my bed before.'

"'Well,' Henderson said of all this, 'I will have to check out your alibis....'

"I don't have to tell you the embarrassment I was facing. In my preconceived scenarios, one of them would have seen that there was no way out, and broken down and confessed to their crime, and I would be hailed as having solved a heinous crime, much like Mr. Holmes. But...I was placed in a precarious and inauspicious situation here."

"So it seems," said someone.

Yes, I thought. Then I spoke. I said, "So neither Mr. Davis nor Mr. Barkley were the felon?"

Willard Reed glared at me for a moment, and said, "No, boy. Both their alibis were solid, concerning the night in question. And this was the cause of my great embarrassment. Two days later, Detective Henderson called on me. He told me that, yes, neither Davis nor Barkley were questionable in the murder. He had talked to both the young ladies whom both men had spent the night with. Both women attested that they had left the party with the men, and had been with them in their rooms all night.

"Thus, my attempt at brilliant amateur detective work went down the sewer pipes. Profusely, and sincerely, I apologized to Henderson for my apparent error. And do you know what he said to me? He said, 'Don't worry.' He said, 'In my line of work, I make these kind of mistakes all the time.' Oh, yes, he said, 'It's part of the job,' but I didn't believe him. I was chagrined. I still am. And thus I give you my contrite story at being a sleuth. I failed miserably. I am...no Sherlock Holmes."

"And so the murder of Carla Black goes unsolved," someone in the group said.

Willard Reed replied, "Yes."

* * * * * * *

It would be a month later that I, too, became somewhat of an amateur detective, or at least involved in Willard Reed's murder mystery. Perhaps "informant" is the correct word.

There was this actress friend of mine, Lisa Jolen. I wished that we could have been more than friends, and I certainly had made my intentions clear to her more than once, until she told me that while she found men to be a distraction at times, she was more interested in women.

I was walking home one early evening and passed the building where Lisa had an apartment. I thought I'd drop in on Lisa. My impromptu visit was inopportune, however, as she was entertaining a female guest. I caught just a glimpse of this guest, who gave me a stern look from within the apartment. The woman was small and blonde and intense-looking. "Let's have lunch tomorrow," Lisa whispered.

I met Lisa for an early lunch the next day. She confessed that she was uncertain about this new love affair. "I keep telling myself that I'll stop getting involved with theater artists," Lisa Jolen said, "but who else am I going to meet? This particular new amorous interest, she's an actress of course. It began so sudden. It was great. But she smothers me. She wants me all to herself, and it's not love. It's obsession, I think. I don't want to be obsessed over. Sometimes, the girl scares me."

"Maybe you should call it off," I suggested.

"Maybe. But Cassandra has quite temper."

"That's her name?"

"Yes. Cassandra Payne." She must have seen it on my face. Lisa said, "What is it?"

"Hm? Oh. I forgot about an errand I have to run."

"Right now?"

"No, no," I said, "something I can take care of later."

I tried to get in contact with Willard Reed, but was unable to. I was afraid he wouldn't be at the next meeting of the Playwright's Chamber, but—much to my relief—he was. I waited until the evening was coming to close, and approached him, asking for a few private words. I quickly told him about my friend and her new lover, and who this lover was.

"So the girl gets around," Reed said, "I don't understand what you're getting at."

"I was thinking of the story you told last month," I said excitedly. "How Ms. Payne was paying close attention to the arguments, and what she said about Carla Black."

Reed raised a brow. "'She's beautiful, she has charisma, she is a great director. She draws people to her, and they fall in love with her.'"

"Yes."

"Good Lord," he said. He was thinking I was thinking.

* * * * * * *

Two days later, Willard Reed invited me to dinner as his guest. He said he had great information for me. I met him at a fine uptown restaurant. I didn't think my suit was good enough to be in such a refined place, but the maitre d' showed me to Reed's table nonetheless.

The man had a bourbon and bitters before him, and was smoking a cigar. He had a pleased expression, like a man just returned from a good safari in the African jungle.

He didn't waste time. "Cassandra Payne murdered Carla Black."

"You know this for sure?"

"She confessed. Right now, she is in the hands of the law."

"I hope you'll tell me everything," I said.

"I plan to. First, a drink?"

"Maybe a little wine."

He waved for a waiter. "You must try the duck here."

"I'm a vegetarian."

"Very good."

After ordering dinner, Mr. Reed went into his narrative. "I went to where The Fritz Shakespeare Ensemble was rehearsing, looking for Ms. Payne. She was there—she wasn't in the next show, but she was holding book for the actors. I asked if I could speak to her alone. I got right to the point. 'You were in love with Carla Black,' I said, 'and you were extremely jealous of her entanglements with Davis and Barkley. I'll venture that you even had a liaison with Ms. Black, and she no longer wanted the affair, just as she was pushing the two men away. You were furious because of this rejection. I saw it on your face when we talked before, but it simply didn't register until now.'

"As I spoke, she was quivering; and when I was done, she burst into tears. She grabbed on to me. I thought she was going to attack me. Instead, she was looking for comfort. She admitted that she did kill Carla Black. It *was* a crime of passion."

"What I don't understand," I said, "is that she was with Bertrand Barkley the night of the murder. She was his alibi, for God's sake!"

"Ah, yes. That thought occurred to me as well, but I had a certain suspicion, which she attested to. Carla Black had left the party early after her confrontations with the men in her life. Ms. Payne followed her, which wasn't long after she had spoken with me. She had a knife with her—it was a costume prop from the show, placed on the belt and never used in any dangerous way, possessing a working, sharp blade nevertheless. Ms. Payne said she had convinced herself she was carrying the knife as protection—it was late, this is New York. But in the back of her mind, she knew she would use it to threaten as an act of love against Carla Black.

"'I really don't know what I was thinking,' she told me in a thicker accent than I remember her having. 'I was seeing red. I was quite inebriated from the Pernod. I was so in love with her. I wanted her to be in my arms forever. She kept telling me what happened between us was a mistake, and that it would never happen again. The same damn thing she told Daniel Davis! We were walking down the street, and she was acting so cold, like she didn't want me near her, like I was trash! I pushed her in an alley, yelling at her. 'You're nothing but a tramp!' I cried, and that's when I took out the knife. I just wanted to scare her, and the next thing I knew, I had the knife in her belly.'

"Looking down at the body of Ms. Black, and realizing what she had done, Ms. Payne ran back to the party. She cleaned the prop knife and put it away. Mr. Barkley was getting quite drunk and making passes at various women. When he came to her, she decided he would suffice as an alibi. She would go home with him. The irony of it! She was believing, by going to Barkley's bed, it would relieve her as a suspect, when—"

"When *she* was relieving *him* as a suspect," I said.

"Indeed."

"So did she think she committed the perfect murder? That she would get off scot-free?"

"She confessed that the guilt was overwhelming and she couldn't live with it anymore. She said she was happy I had figured her out. She even said she'd been contemplating going to the police and turning herself in. 'Now would be a good time to do such,' I informed her. 'I will go with you, if you'd like.'

"She nodded. She got her coat, and I escorted her to the station. To be honest, I just wanted to see the smug look on Detective Henderson's face. I may have made a fool out of myself before in my novice notions of being a sleuth, but I was now delivering the murderess straight into hands. And now here we are."

"You solved the murder of Carla Black," I said, "you should feel proud."

"Pah!" he laughed. "I did nothing. Without your tip, I would've still been the bumbling fool. Needless to say, I was foolish enough to confront Ms. Payne the way I did. Despite circumstantial suspicion, what if she was not the culprit? Or what if she felt no remorse and denied the crime? She simply could have laughed in my face and called me insane. She could have tarnished my image in the theater community, claiming I was going around and accusing everybody of murder!"

"But that wasn't the case."

"No. Blind, dumb luck was on my side."

A waiter arrived with our food.

"Time for dinner," Reed said. He raised his glass of bourbon. "Here's to two playwright/detectives."

I raised my wine glass. "Playwrights."

CAMPUS SEX CIRCLE

GRAHAM & PESHA

Pesha says to Graham, "You need furniture," and leans against the red brick wall of the loft.

"Just moved in," Graham says.

"You said you've been here three weeks."

"Three weeks is nothing."

"A table would be nice."

"Who needs a table."

"I can think of things to do with a table," Pesha says. She smiles, and he smiles back. He goes to her and it doesn't appear that she's going to stop him. He kisses her. They hug. They kiss some more. She's forty-three and he's twenty-five. He's a graduate student and she's a tenured professor.

He says, "You should've come by sooner."

"I couldn't."

"I missed you."

Pesha moves away from Graham. She paces around the empty loft. "Okay," she says. "Okay. So. So I'm leaving him."

"I knew you would."

"You don't know anything."

"Did you tell him?"

"No. I made this decision two hours ago."

"I see."

"Then I called you."

"You're going to tell him?"

"Tonight. I hope."

"You'll need a place to stay. You can stay here."

"I'm not staying here," she says.

"You're leaving him for me," he says.

Pesha looks irritated. "No. I'm *leaving* him for *me.*"

Graham goes to her, but she moves away.

She says, "I had sex with Tom last night."

"You also had sex with me," he says.

"Not last night."

"Yesterday."

"I had sex with him after I was with you," she says.

"Oh, I see."

"I know that sounds bad."

"Well," he says. "Yeah."

"We had sex in my office. I had sex with him at home, in bed. Two separate realities. You understand."

"That's how you like to look at it."

She nods. "Yes."

"Why are you telling me this?"

"Does it bother you?"

He says, "You know it does."

"Tell me about the girls you fuck," she says. "Ask if it bothers me. Tell me. Tell me about their breasts, their tits. Tell me about their smell; and tell me about their necks, their hair, their eyes. Ask if it bothers me."

"There are no girls."

"Why don't I believe you," she says.

"So you had sex with your husband last night," Graham says. "Do pontificate, my dear."

"All day I was thinking about it, and I didn't want to think about it," Pesha says. "I have more important things to think about, like my new book. But all I could think about was sex. Sex with Tom and how I didn't care for it. How I abhor it. I haven't had sex with him the last two months, except last night."

"What brought it on?"

"He did. All I wanted to do was go home and work on my book. Tom had other ideas. He'd had two glasses of wine—he tends to get rather randy after two glasses of wine," Pesha says.

"And so he was," Graham says.

"And so he was. He wanted to get me into bed. I figured: well, why not."

"Why not."

"It was nothing exciting," she says. "You'd like an exciting story, full of kinky sex and debauchery."

"I like details."

"He got on top of me and it was over in a matter of minutes."

"That's quite a story."

"You're not listening to me."

"'It was over in a matter of minutes,' she said."

"It was the missionary position," Pesha says. "You know how I hate the missionary position."

"Um-hm."

"I started thinking—today—I started thinking how Tom and I *always* have sex in that damn position. He doesn't like me to get on top. He doesn't like me on my stomach. He doesn't even like me bent over a table the way you do me in my office."

They look at each other. It's very quiet in the loft. Somewhere in some shaft, some wind is howling.

"So you're leaving him," Graham says.

"I've been married to him for twelve years," Pesha says. "Twelve goddamn years and I can't stand another year. I have to get out. And what will our colleagues in the department say?"

"Do you care?"

"People talk. You know what the department is like. All that nasty gossip."

"Do you think Tom has ever had an affair?"

"No. No, he has not."

"How do you know?"

"He hasn't."

"All those pretty young girls in his classes."

"He doesn't notice."

"I don't believe that," Graham says.

"You notice them."

He shrugs. "I've seen them around."

"What are they like," she says, "when you screw them?"

Graham is about to say something and Pesha stops him with a wave of her hand. She sits down on the futon, the only piece of furniture in the loft, except a white plastic lawn chair.

Graham sits in the white plastic lawn chair and says, "I do need furniture."

"You don't understand how frightening this is," Pesha says.

"It doesn't have to be."

"My whole world could fall apart. I don't like change, Graham. And at the same time: I embrace it, because I know it's what I need."

"I'll be there for you."

"Where?"

"What?"

"You said 'there.'"

"Here," he says. "If you need me, you know. I'm here."

"That's what scares me," she says. "Needing you. I don't *want* to need you. There's no reason for it. I shouldn't need *any*one. I *don't* need anyone. I believe I can handle this by myself."

"Oh."

"It's not you," she says. "Why I'm leaving him. You know this."

"No."

"There have been others."

"Others?"

"Students."

"Oh."

"Just two, really."

"Oh," he says.

"I never told you this. No, I guess I did not."

"No."

"There was no reason to."

"There wasn't."

"But I'll tell you now."

"Okay."

"I mean, why not?"

"Why not."

"Today is my day to come clean."

"Confess your sins to me, my child."

"Stop that! One of them was nothing—it was brief," Pesha says. "The second one—well, that one lasted a few months. Two months. Maybe one and a half months."

"Six weeks."

"Maybe seven," she says. "He was accepted into a very good Ph.D. program far away. It was for the best. You want a Ph.D., too."

"I'm not sure."

"Get one. They're good for you."

"You want me to leave the university," Graham says.

"Eventually."

"Can I ask you something?"

"Of course."

"Did you ever love Tom?"

"I still love Tom. It's a fucked-up love. Listen to the way I've been talking. These words—they sound so alien. I never say 'fuck' unless you're around. You're a bad influence." She smiles.

"I'm a rude host," Graham says; he also smiles. "Would you like something to drink?" he asks.

"A glass of Chablis would be nice."

"That I can do."

Graham goes to the area that's a kitchen—there's a sink and fridge there, anyway. Graham pours two glasses of wine. Pesha looks around the loft. She sees something on the floor: a condom packet, unopened. She gets up from the futon and sits on the white plastic lawn chair. Graham hands her a glass of wine.

"Thank you," she says.

"Cheers?"

"To?"

"New beginnings?"

"Let's not start uttering platitudes, my dear."

"I like platitudes," he says.

He sits down on the futon. She joins him. They sip wine. She picks up the condom packet and says, "For me?"

"Sure."

"We never use them."

"They're good to have around," he says.

They kiss.

ASHLEY

Ashley is walking down the street, looking for an address. She's looking for the building where her sister Andrea lives. She carries two bags: one with her clothes, the other with her laptop. She's deeply tanned, has assorted tattoos and piercings, and is nineteen-years-old. She finds the building she's looking for and goes in. This is the same building where Graham lives. She goes up the stairs and finds a door with "311" on it. She takes out her keys, unlocks the door, and goes in.

She says, "Andrea?"

No one is here. There's a futon on the floor. Ashley is very tired. She strips to her panties and socks and goes to sleep on the futon.

ASHLEY & GRAHAM

The problem is: Ashley's in the wrong loft. Graham comes home and discovers her. He's not alone. Judy is with him. Judy is twenty-three and also a graduate student. Graham and Judy have been out having a bite to eat and a lot to drink. They want to have sex; Graham has brought Judy here for that purpose.

Graham turns the lights on and Judy looks around and says, "You really *don't* have furniture."

"I'm a minimalist," Graham says.

Ashley wakes up. She sits up and says, "Andrea?"

Judy says, "Who the hell is that?"

Graham says, "Who is what?"

"The girl in your bed," Judy says.

"The girl...in my bed."

It's like one of those comic moments in movies.

Ashley says, "Are you Andrea's friends?"

"Excuse me," Graham says, "who are you?"

"Yeah, right," Judy says, making her way out the door.

"Where are you going?" Graham says.

"I don't know what you had in mind," Judy says, "but I'm not into it."

"I don't know who she is," he says, "I've never seen her before!"

But Judy is gone, saying, "Asshole, asshole, asshole."

Graham turns to Ashley. Ashley is covering her breasts with the blanket.

"Hi," Ashley says, and smiles.

"You want to tell me who you are?"

"Ashley."

"Okay, Ashley, do you want to tell me what you're doing in my bed, and my home?"

"This is my sister's place."

"This is *not* your sister's place."

"It has to be. My sister is Andrea—most people call her Andi. She calls me Ash. Andi and Ash. What's your name?"

"Graham."

"Like the cracker?"

"Are you intentionally trying to antagonize me?" he asks.

"Where's Andrea?"

"Who?"

"My sister!"

"There is no Andrea here," Graham says.

"This is 722 Silver, right?"

"Yes."

"That's the address my sister gave me. She sent me a key in the mail. Number 411."

"This is 311."

"Oh shit," Ashley says.

What happened was that Ashley was so tired, she just flew in from Europe, she thought 311 was 411. Why the key opened the door is a mystery, but Ashley got in, and fell asleep.

"Look," Ashley says, "I'm sorry."

"It's okay," Graham says.

"I hope this didn't mess anything up with your girlfriend."

"She's not my girlfriend."

Ashley grabs her shirt and puts it on. She's doesn't seem to mind that Graham gets a look of her tanned, small breasts. She reaches into one of her bags and pulls out a comic book. She hands the comic book to Graham and says, "Here. This is for you. I want to give this to you."

He takes the comic book. It's called *Frog & Elephant, Ph.D.* It's in black and white panels.

"It's cool," Ashley says, "you'll like it."

"Yeah?"

"I mean, it's mine."

"Well, if it's yours—"

"Now it's yours."

Graham doesn't know what to say. He says, "Thank you."

"You probably want me to go, right?"

"Yes."

Ashley gathers her two bags. "My sister is going to love this story."

* * * * * * *

Ashley returns a few minutes later. Graham is reading the comic book.

"My sister isn't there and the key doesn't seem to work," she says.

GRAHAM & ASHLEY

Ashley is the writer and artist for *Frog & Elephant, Ph.D.s*. It's published by a small press in New Jersey. It's about, yes, a frog and an elephant who hang out with each other and have adventures. They both have various Ph.D.s in numerous fields.

Graham and Ashley order pizza. Ashley is very hungry. They drink beers and sit on the floor of the loft and talk.

Graham asks her, "What made you get into comic books?"

"Ever since I was nine, I wanted to be a superhero," Ashley says.

"In a spandex suit?"

"Bright and shiny colors!"

"So what happened?"

"Reality interfered," she says. "I saw a kid getting beat up by a bunch of bullies. He was your basic nerd, this kid. Thick glasses, always reading books, in the chess club."

"Sounds like me."

"Skinny and pale."

"Not me."

"I tried to save him. I tried to be the superhero. But the bullies just beat me up too."

"Ouch."

"Ouch is right. So this kid and me, we both had bloody lips, black eyes. I helped him up. We were both limping. I walked home with him. That's when I fell in love. His name was Randy."

Graham laughs. "Randy!"

"And was he ever!" Ashley says. "Just kidding. We were nine. Ten. Something like that. The silent, secret, stolen kisses—just pecks really. We're not talking tongues. Scary. New. Sexy. Wow. Hey," she says, "you look sleepy."

"I am. It's late."

"Are you sure it's okay that I sleep here?"

"Where you going to go?"

"I have money. I have a credit card. I can get a hotel room."

"No. That's silly."

"Thanks," Ashley says, softly.

"But," he says, "I only have this one bed."

"I can sleep on the floor," she says. "I've slept on many floors, believe me."

"Well, okay."

"Graham?"

"Yeah?"

"Is there any reason why you don't want me to share your bed with you?" she asks. "You don't have, like, a serious girlfriend, do you? Or are you gay? Which is all right. You know."

"I don't have a serious girlfriend," he says, amused, "and I'm not gay."

"Oh. I guess I was feeling a little rejected here."

"We don't know each other."

"Story of my life."

"I'm too old for you."

"Stop making excuses," she says. She's serious. "If you think I'm too ugly to fuck, just tell me."

Graham says, "I just think it'd be a bad idea."

She says, "I like bad ideas."

ASHLEY & PESHA

Ashley is listening to music on the CD player, wearing a green tank top and red shorts. There's a knock on the door. She answers the door. Pesha is there. Pesha comes in, pushing Ashley aside.

Pesha looks at Ashley and says, "Well."

"Hi."

"Is Graham here?"

"No," Ashley says.

"Are you his girlfriend?"

"No," Ashley says. She holds her hand out to Pesha, but Pesha just looks at it with disgust.

"Fuck you," Pesha says, "you little bitch."

"Hey," Ashley says, shocked.

"Where is he?"

"He went out to the store."

"I really feel stupid," Pesha says, closing her eyes and sighing.

Graham walks in, holding a grocery bag. "Hi, Pesha," he says.

"Hello," Pesha says, a whisper.

"I see you, uh, met Ashley."

"Bastard," Pesha says. "I trusted you. Why the hell did I trust you?"

"He can explain," Ashley says.

"Forget this," Pesha says, and walks out the door.

"Crap," Graham says.

"Go after her," Ashley says, "before it's too late."

He gives her the grocery bag, and he goes.

PESHA & GRAHAM

They sit in a small pub. There's a college atmosphere about the place. The table they sit at is in the corner and round and very small. They're both drinking beers. Graham explains Ashley, but he leaves out that he fucked the girl last night.

"You really expect me to buy this tale?" Pesha says.

"I let her stay because she had nowhere to go," Graham says. "I'm sure her sister will show up soon."

"She was half naked when she opened the door."

"She's a free spirit," he says. "Hell, she's a kid."

Pesha takes a drink from her beer bottle. "I told him. Finally. And I left him."

"I know."

"How?"

"A feeling. Do you need a place to stay?"

"Do I want to shack up with you and the kid?" she says. "I have a hotel room for now."

"Really?"

"At the Marriott. It's rather nice."

"I'd love to see it."

She says, "I'm still mad at you."

He smiles. "No you're not."

She smiles. "No—I'm not."

* * * * * * *

They go to the Marriott. Graham stays the night.

ASHLEY & TOM

It's night. Ashley is in the loft, listening to music, working on her laptop. There's a knock on the door. She's still in the tank top and the tight shorts. She opens the door. A tall, slender man in his forties stands there. He's in a jacket and tie, rumpled; he looks worried. His longish hair is gray-white.

Ashley smiles. "Hello."

"Are you his girlfriend?" the man asks. He's Tom Goldberg, Pesha's husband.

"What?"

"Is this the residence of Graham Marcus?"

"Yes," Ashley says.

"Is he here?"

"No," Ashley says.

He walks in, pushing her aside.

"Hey!" she says.

"This place isn't even furnished," he says.

"It's post-postmodern."

He turns and looks at her. "What did you say?"

"Who are you?"

"What do you know about post-modernism?"

"Lots," Ashley says.

"Is she here?"

"Who?"

"My wife."

"No."

"Her name is Pesha. Do you know her?"

"No."

"And who are you?"

"Ashley."

"Are you his girlfriend?"

"My sister lives upstairs," she says, "but she's not there."

"Huh?"

"Who are *you?"*

"Tom Goldberg," he says. "Dr. Tom Goldberg."

"I think—"

"I checked with the registrar," he says. "I was given this address."

"So why would your wife be here?"

"Because she left me, and she said she was sleeping with Graham Marcus."

"Oh," Ashley says, nodding. "I see."

"You know something," Tom says.

"No. I don't."

"I can see it in your eyes," he says, moving towards her.

She backs away from him. "There's nothing in my eyes."

"Tell me," he says.

"Tell you what?"

"Tell me what you know."

"I don't know anything."

"Then tell me what you don't know."

TOM & ASHLEY

Ashley sits on the floor, her tanned legs crossed. Tom sits in the white lawn chair, his tie loosened. Tom keeps looking at her legs and her tits, and she's quite aware of this.

"I don't she's coming back," Ashley says. "The both of them. He or she."

"So tell me again," he says. "Tell me what happened."

"I told you three times."

"I'm trying to get a clear picture in my head."

"I answered the door," she says, "and there was—"

"Pesha."

"Yes."

"She was looking for him."

"That's what she said. She thought I was his girlfriend."

"But you're not."

"I just met him."

"Your sister lives upstairs."

"Yes."

"But she's not here."

"I have no idea where she is," Ashley says.

"And they left together."

"No. She stormed out. She seemed upset. He went after her."

"He'll come back," Tom says. "What do you intend to do? Punch him out?"

"I want to know the truth."

"Do you know what I think?"

He looks away. "I can't wait to hear it."

"I think it's been over between you and your wife for a long time now."

Tom nods. "Maybe."

"Maybe," Ashley says, "it's time to let go."

"I love her."

"Do you really?"

"But she doesn't love me. It's like, I don't know. Like we're brother and sister."

This touches Ashley. "Don't look so sad, Mr. Tom Goldberg."

"Do I look sad?" he says. "I feel sad. I thought it was anger. But it's sadness."

"Do you want a beer?" she asks. "I think you need a beer."

"Yes," he says, "please."

She goes and gets him a beer. He watches her. She gets a beer too. She gives him a beer and says, "So what do you teach?"

"Let's not talk about me anymore. Let's talk about you. You're a student here?"

"I'm starting next quarter."

"Freshman?"

"Yeah."

"Majoring in—?"

She shrugs.

"Come on," he says.

"Maybe business."

"Really?"

"I know. Here I am, an artist...."

"An artist!"

"I do this comic book," she says. "Here," and she finds an issue of *Frog & Elephant*, gives it to him.

"This is yours?"

"Issue four will be out next month," she says. "The fan base is growing. I plan on *Frog & Elephant* to be a huge franchise in the next ten, fifteen years. Large print runs, a weekly cartoon TV series, maybe a feature movie, merchandise, you name it."

"Hence the business degree."

"Bingo, baby."

"And if this comic book doesn't work out, you'll still have that degree to fall back on."

"It'll work out," she says, "I can feel it in my bones."

"You have to have faith," Tom says, nodding. "That's good. Too many people don't chase their dreams. There was a time I wanted to be a poet. I wrote poetry. But I gave it up. Now I'm a literary critic, a vile thing."

They sip their beers and look at each other.

"What are you thinking about?" Ashley asks.

"My wife. I can't help it."

"It's okay."

"We're not in love anymore," he says. "I don't know when it stopped. We used to be very much in love, but that was many years ago."

"Love is nice."

"Have you ever really been in love? You're so young."

"Sure," Ashley says. "Do you and Pesha have children?"

"No. She never wanted any. I did."

"Really?"

"Oh yes. It's too late now. I thought when Pesha got older, her maternal instinct would kick in."

"I want kids," Ashley says. "Two, maybe three."

"Two or three sounds nice. I doubt I'm going to find anyone who'd want to have my babies."

"I'd have your baby."

Tom doesn't seem to hear that. "What I'm afraid of," he says, "is being alone. Pesha goes, and I don't think I'll fall in love again."

"Why do you think that?"

"I'm forty-three years old."

"What does age have to do with anything?" Ashley says. "You're an attractive man."

"God, I'd love to kiss you," Tom says.

Pesha & Graham & Tom & Ashley & Andrea Too

Graham and Pesha enter the loft and find Tom and Ashley making love on the futon.

"Oh boy," Graham says.

"Hi guys," Ashley says.

"Tom?!?" Pesha says.

"Hello, Pesha," Tom says.

"Okay, before everyone loses their cool," Graham says, "we should all talk about this."

"That's a good idea," Tom says.

"I'm game," Ashley says.

"I'm leaving," Pesha says.

"No, don't, please," says Tom.

Pesha says, "Would you both put your clothes on for Pete's sake!"

"Do you have something against the naked body?" Tom says. "It's natural and beautiful."

"Are you on drugs?" Pesha says.

"I wish," Tom says.

"I will *not* stay here and talk if you two insane people are naked," Pesha says.

Tom and Ashley get dressed.

"Oh," Pesha says very softly, "this is a bad dream, isn't it?"

"If this were a porno," Graham says, "the four of us would be getting it on right now." He laughs. He's trying to lighten the air.

"Graham," Pesha says very seriously, "shut up. I'm trying to cope with the fact that I just walked in on my husband having sex with a child!"

"She's hardly a child," Tom says.

"She's younger than you, by how many generations?"

Tom says, "Might I point out to you that you walked in on me inside your boyfriend's apartment? And that you are in the company of said boyfriend?"

"I just broke up with him," Pesha says.

"You did?" says Graham.

Tom says, "Might I point out that you recently left me, asking for a divorce?"

"I changed my mind," Pesha says.

"I decided to write poetry again, just today. Do you know what that means, Pesha?"

There's a knock at the door.

"Now what?" Pesha says.

A young woman with blonde hair is at the door. "I'm looking for my sister."

"Andi!" Ashley says.

"Ash!" the young woman with blonde hair at the door says.

The two embrace.

"Who are all these people?" Ashley's sister asks.

"Well," Ashley says.

"You should've gotten here five minutes earlier," Pesha says. She sways, like she might fall.

"Are you all right?" Graham asks.

"I just need to sit down and catch my breath," Pesha says.

SHAME PEEPER

My girlfriend, Erin, and I are having an argument—she says I'm lazy, she says I need to get a job; she says she hates it when she has to pay the full rent for the month.

She's right. I am lazy. I haven't been feeling like going to work, lately.

"You were fired twice in one month!" she says.

"You're right," I say.

"What are we going to do about this?" she says.

"I don't know," I say.

"Maybe you should move out," she says.

"If I move out, you'll still be paying all the rent," I say.

"You should move out," she says; "it'll teach you a lesson."

"What lesson?" I ask.

"About loss," she says.

"You mean you're kicking me out," I say.

"I don't want to do that," she says, "I want you to move out on your own."

"Have some balls," I say, "and kick me out."

"I'm not going to kick you out," she says.

"Do you really want me to go?" I say.

"I want *some*thing to happen," she says.

There's a knock on the door.

We look at each other.

Another knock.

"Don't answer it," she whispers.

"Don't be silly," I say, going to answer the door.

"Saved by the bell," Erin says.

It's Dave, my friend Dave. "*Dave*," I say, "what's going on?"

"I was out for a walk," he says, "I was walking by, and I thought I'd just—well, just drop by. Say hi."

"Come in," I say, knowing that this is something Erin doesn't want.

"Hey," Dave says.

Erin smiles real friendly like and says, "Hey, Dave, how are you doing?"

"Well," he says, "well, I'm not sure."

"What's up?" I say.

He says, "I was just walking by."

"So you said."

"What's happening with you two?" he says.

"Well," I say, "well, I'm not sure."

"Not much," my girlfriend says. "Would you like a beer?"

"Sure," Dave says.

"I'd like a beer too," I say.

Erin gives me a look—you know the kind of look—and goes to the kitchen.

"Sit down," I say to Dave.

He sits down.

Erin returns with three beers.

"Thanks," Dave says.

"Thanks," I say.

Erin drinks her beer and looks at us.

"Nice night," I say.

"It's a little cold out there," he says.

"Yeah," I say.

"Are you still seeing Bonnie?" Erin asks him.

"Oh yes," he says, "of course. Yes."

"Well," I say.

"I was thinking," Dave says.

"Yes?"

He says to my girlfriend, "Would you do a Tarot card reading for me?"

"Sure," she says.

She used to work as a professional telephone Tarot reader for two years—before I met her, when she used to be married to someone else. She's not married to this someone else anymore, of course; she lives with me. Or I live with her.

"You don't mind?" Dave says.

"No," she lies.

"That last reading you gave me," he says, "well, it was right on the money."

"I like to do readings," she says. She gets up and gets her cards. She hands the cards to Dave and tells him to shuffle.

I watch him shuffle. My girlfriend and I look at each other. I remember the first time she gave me a Tarot reading; it was the first night we slept together. That was a little over a year ago. It feels like ten years ago.

Dave says okay and gives her the deck of cards back.

She cuts the deck, and lays the cards out on the table before us.

"Hmm—interesting," she says, brushing a few strands of her brunette hair out of her eyes..

"Yeah?" Dave says.

"Yeah," she says. "There's some big changes coming along. Little by little, one change after another, growing into one huge one."

"Yeah?"

"Yeah," she says.

"Cool," he says.

My girlfriend yawns and I think it's a fake yawn. She says she feels sleepy and she's going to go to bed.

"Good night," Dave says. "Thanks for the reading."

Before going to bed, she gives me a look—you know the kind of look. She usually falls asleep fast and I find myself glad that she has decided to go to sleep. We'll have to discuss the matter of my leaving at some other date. I think she'll forget about it tomorrow, maybe bring it up a week later. That's what always happens.

Dave and I have a few more beers and we talk about books and things and then he goes, "Hey, let's go drink some Jim Beam."

I'm all for that.

We leave the apartment and walk down to his place, a few blocks away. There, we drink Jim Beam and listen to Pink Floyd on the CD player. We get pretty drunk. Things are spinning, like a record.

It's three A.M.

Dave asks me if I might marry my girlfriend some day and I tell him I don't know.

"Why is that?"

"I don't know," I say. I want to tell him what my girlfriend wants me to do, that she wants me to leave, but I'm not drunk enough to do that.

"She's pretty," Dave says.

"Yeah," I say.

"She's very good with those Tarot cards," Dave says.

"Yeah," I say.

"Because she's right," Dave says, "she had it right on the nose—there are big changes coming for me. Real big changes."

"Yeah?" I say.

"I haven't told anyone this," Dave says, "but Bonnie's pregnant."

"Yeah?" I say.

"Yeah," he says.

"No shit," I say.

"No shit," he says with a smile.

"How far gone is she?" I ask.

"Two months," he says.

"That's something else," I say.

"It is," he says. "I wasn't sure what I was going to do, but now I know. After that Tarot reading, now I know. I'm going to marry Bonnie."

"Yeah?"

"Yeah," he says. "I'm going to marry her and we're going to be a family."

"That's something else," I say.

"It is," he says. "Who would ever thought? Me. Me, a husband and a father. Did you ever think I could do such a thing?"

"Well," I say, "no."

"No," he says. "But I can. I will. This is good."

"Yeah," I say.

We're drunk all right, weaving about as we stand there and talk.

"I have this great vision right now," Dave says, holding the Jim Beam bottle loosely in his hand. He goes, "Four or five months from now. Bonnie's stomach is huge. I reach down and touch her stomach. And the baby kicks. The baby kicks so hard that my hand hurts. *Now, is that something else, or is that something else?*"

"Something weird happened this morning," I say.

"Yeah?" Dave says.

"Yeah," I say, drinking more Jim Beam. I've had too much as it is, and it's hard to speak.

"So what happened?"

"Erin was in the shower this morning," I say, "and I hear her let out this scream, a small scream, a yelp really. I go into the bathroom and I'm like, 'What is it?' She says, 'There was a head peeping in on me through the window.'"

"A head?"

"A Peeping Tom."

"No shit," Dave says.

"She's like the head disappeared when she yelled at it. She yelled, 'What the hell do you think you're doing?' She says the head was wearing a baseball cap. She says the head was a small head. I run out back to see if this small head with the baseball cap is still there. You know, we have that alley in the back where the bathroom window is."

"Yeah."

"And I find our two white lawn chairs that we have back there stacked on top of each other, right under the bathroom window."

"No shit," Dave says.

"No shit," I say. "But the alley is empty, no one's around. Erin's out of the shower when I go back in. She's not scared, she's pissed. 'No one's out there,' I tell her, and she's like, 'I know what I saw,' and I'm like, 'I believe you' and she's: 'I think I know who it was.' 'Who?' 'Andy,' she says."

"Andy?" Dave says.

"He's the apartment manager," I say, "and he's like seventy-three years old."

"I think I've seen the old fart," Dave says.

"Yeah, old," I say, "and five foot three."

"A little man," Dave says.

"That's what Erin said. 'That dirty little man,' she said this morning. 'Are you sure it was him?' I asked and she was: 'I couldn't make a positive ID, but I'm pretty sure. Who has a little head like that?'"

"Wow," Dave says.

"This all makes sense," I say, "because I'm pretty sure that Andy wants to fuck her."

"Who could blame him," Dave says. "You have a pretty girlfriend."

"Well," I say, "yeah."

"You say this guy is seventy-three?"

"Or older."

Dave says, "I didn't know men that old still have interest in sex."

"Viagra," I say. "Which is a funny thing—not really funny, more like messed-up—but when Erin first moved in there (before I was living with her) this Andy guys kind of slyly says to her, 'I have a whole bottle of Viagra in my cabinet that I'm just itching to use.'"

"Hey," Dave says, "the question is: is it sexual harassment yet?"

"That's what I said. But Erin said, 'He was kidding.' 'He wasn't kidding.' 'No,' she goes, 'he was just joking.' But I think she knows, now, what he was suggesting."

"That's fucked-up," Dave says.

"Yeah," I say.

"Hey," Dave says, "so the question is: are you going to do something about it?"

"I'm going to," I say.

"Good," he says. "Good."

* * * * * * *

Erin is in on it with me: we set Andy up. I have the camcorder in hand and ready, Erin is in the shower and singing. I'm waiting in the kitchen, where I have a good view of the side of the apartment where the bathroom window is. My girlfriend showers for five minutes and sure enough, the little old fart shows up. He wears that baseball cap he always has on. He looks around, he seems nervous. He climbs on top of the stacked lawn chairs. I resist the urge to rush out. I'm slow and quiet instead. I have the camcorder to my eye. I have him now, I have him on tape. I move in closer. He's peering into the window. Steam and Erin's out-of-tune singing float out of the window like small dreams.

"Hey, Andy," I say, "good view?"

He's startled, of course. He turns and looks at me.

I say, "Smile, you."

He goes, "Ahh," and the chairs tumble. He falls to the ground. "You bastard," he says, "you fucking bastard."

"I got you," I say.

"You *bastard,*" he says.

Erin is outside now, wearing a robe. "We caught you, you dirty old man!" she says.

"I'm hurt," he says.

"Good," Erin says, "you deserve it."

"You hurt me," he says.

"You hurt yourself," I say.

"You were peeping on me!" Erin says.

"I was not," Andy says, "I was just looking at the water drain, it needs fixing—"

"Bull," Erin says, "bull-oney."

"Fuck you," he says, "you bitch."

Erin's like, "What?!?"

"Hey," I say, "you're on camera."

"That's right," Erin says, "we have you on *camera*. We're going to show this tape to the landlord!"

Andy gets on his feet and points a bony finger. "Go ahead, you—you—you—you—"

"You'll get fired," I say.

"I don't care," Andy says. "You—you—"

"We'll show it to the police!" Erin says.

"Oh yeah?" Andy says, adjusting his thick glasses. "Show it to them, I don't care, you—*you.*"

"What you did is illegal," she says, "you'll go to jail."

"I don't care," he says, *"you bitch."*

"Don't you call me a bitch," Erin says.

"You're a stuck-up bitch," Andy says, "swaying your little ass and bouncing your little tits like you were something hot. You know what, you're *nothing!* Nothing! Screw you! Screw the both of you weirdos," he says, walking away.

Erin and I go inside. Our hearts are beating fast. We laugh nervously.

"That was something else," I say.

"That was crazy," she says.

"Wow," I say.

"We got him," she says, "we got him."

"Yeah," I say, turning the camcorder off.

Twenty minutes later, I walk Erin out to her car. Andy comes after us, or me. He appears from nowhere; maybe he was waiting behind a bush. He has a metal pipe in his hand. He yells, "I'm going to bash your head in you—you—you—motherfucker!"

Erin screams.

Andy takes a swing at me with the pipe. He's old, it's easy to get out of the way. I'm no fighter, but I punch him in the face. I hit him hard. He falls back to the ground, spitting out teeth and blood. He begins to weep.

"You're a dead man," he says.

"You stupid man," I say.

"You've made a big mistake," he says.

"No, you did," I say.

"You hurt me," he says.

"You wanted to hurt *me,*" I say.

"Is that how you get off?" he says. "Hurting old people?"

Then the police show up.

The cops separate the three of us and get our stories. I tell the officer questioning me everything that happened. I show him the camcorder. "I have it all on tape," I say.

He's younger than me, this cop. He nods and writes down what I say in a small notepad.

I hear Andy, his voice high-pitched and loud: "I'm a senior citizen, goddammit! I'm old and senile and I don't know what I'm doing! That doesn't give him the excuse to knock me on the ground! This is elder abuse!"

The cops want to see the tape. I go inside with two of them, connect the camcorder to the TV and show them the evidence.

"Well, he's a Peeping Tom, all right," one cop says.

"Are you going to arrest him?" I ask.

"Here's the thing," the second cop says, "we really don't want to arrest a man his age."

"What?" I say.

"Guys like him die in jail and it makes us look bad."

"You're going to let him get away with it?" I say.

"Here's the other thing," the second cop says. "We're going to have to take you downtown and book you."

"What?" I say.

"You physically assaulted him."

"It was self-defense!"

"Look, we know that," the first cop says, "and I'm sure the D.A. will agree. Worse scenario: it goes to trial but I'm sure a jury will agree with you. The problem is, we're bound by duty to charge any person who physically assaults another, no matter the circumstance. The fact he's a senior citizen doesn't help."

"This is crazy," I say. "If it were the other way around, if I'd done what he did, you guys would have me hog-tied right now."

The cops don't look at me.

The third cop comes in and says, "I read the old man his rights and cuffed him. He's in my car."

The other cops look at him.

"Look," the third cop says, "if we're going to charge this guy, we have to charge the old timer. He had a lead pipe in his hand."

The first cop sighs. "Okay, Steve, but if the old guy has a heart attack or something, you're taking the heat."

The second cop takes out his handcuffs.

"Is that necessary?" I say.

"It's procedure," he says apologetically.

Erin walks into the apartment, sees what's happening, and goes, "What is *this?* Why are you arresting him?"

"Procedure, ma'am," the third cop says.

Erin looks at me and says, "This is just great."

"I'm sorry," I say.

"I guess I'll have to post your bail," she says.

"No need, ma'am," the first cop says. "We're taking him down to the substation to charge and book him. Then we'll release him on his own recognizance. He'll receive a notice in the mail when to go to court. The whole matter takes an hour or two, at most."

"And what about that pervert?" she says. "That peeper?"

"He's being charged too," the third cop says.

"And released?" she says.

"No, ma'am. He'll stay in, unless he meets bail. He'll be charged with the peeping and attempted assault and battery."

Erin looks at me and shakes her head.

"It'll be all right," I say as I'm led out of the apartment.

Erin goes, "That's what you *always* say."

* * * * * * *

So I take a taxi cab back to the apartment after I'm booked and released at the police substation downtown. It's a $7 fare and I have $8 on me. I wonder what I'm going to eat today since I now don't have any money.

Erin's there. I'm surprised. She's watching TV, wearing pink shorts and a white T-shirt.

"What are you doing home?" I ask.

"What do you mean?" she says. "What kind of question is that?"

"Shouldn't you be at work?"

She says, "How could I possibly go to work after what happened this morning?"

"I took a cab," I say. "If I knew you were here, I would've asked you to come pick me up."

"Why didn't you call?"

"I didn't think you were home."

"Like I could *really* go to work and concentrate on all the bull-shit *there,*" she says.

"Hi, honey, I'm home," I say.

She sighs. She stands up. She hugs me. She kisses me lightly on the lips. "I'm acting like a doofus. I'm glad you're back. I'm sorry about what happened. Was it horrible in jail?"

"It wasn't jail. They took me to this building on 14th Street, down into the basement; they finger-printed me, took my mug shot, charged me, had me sign some papers, gave me a coffee and donut, and let me go."

"They didn't give you a *donut,*" she says.

"They did," I said. "A plain glazed, round donut."

She laughs. "The cops gave you a *donut.*"

"I was hungry."

"Where are these papers you signed?"

The papers are folded in my back pocket. I show them to her.

I say this: "That one cop told me the D.A. might not pursue the charges, once they examine the facts of the case."

"Was Andy there too?" she asks.

"No. I think they took him to the actual jail."

She says, "Good." She says, "He belongs there."

I agree.

"Do you want to have sex?" she says. "I really feel like having sex," she says.

"Sure," I say, "why not."

We haven't had sex in a while.

* * * * * * *

The landlord comes by later that day. His name is Mr. Baumberger. He's very tall and thin and has white hair. I think he's in his late fifties. He wears a thick gold chain around his neck, a Hawaiian shirt, and tinted prescription glasses.

He knocks on the door and Erin says, "Don't answer it."

"Why not?" I say.

"It's bad news," she says, "I just know it."

"I'm not going to live that way."

"Then I'll answer it," she says. "I'll show you: I can be brave as anyone else." She opens the door. "Mr. Baumberger," she says.

"Can I come in?" he says.

"Sure," Erin says. She gives me a nervous glance.

"I heard about what happened this morning," he says, "and I must say, I'm not happy."

"We're not happy either," my girlfriend says.

"Andy has lived here and worked for me for ten years," he says. "Nothing like this has ever happened."

"I'm sure he's done it before," I say.

"I don't think so," Mr. Baumberger says. "You two must have done something to set him off."

"*We* didn't do anything," she says. "He was looking in on me while I showered, and then he tried to kill my boyfriend with a metal pipe."

"It's just so hard to believe," the landlord says.

"We have it on video tape," I say.

"Really? Can I see that tape?"

I show him the tape.

His face goes pale when he watches the tape. He says, "Is this the original?"

"It's a copy," I said. "I gave the original to the police."

"Can I have this copy?"

"No," Erin says, "you can't."

I'm surprised by her reaction. I say to the landlord, "I can make you a copy."

He clears his throat. "This is very unfortunate."

"He's a friend of yours, isn't he?" Erin says.

He doesn't look us. "I'm afraid I'm going to have to ask you both to move."

I'm not expecting this; nor is Erin. Erin goes, "What?" and I'm like, "What?"

"Preferably, I'd like you to move as soon as possible, tomorrow," Mr. Baumberger says. "Legally, I can't demand that. Just to keep to procedure, I'll have a 30-Day Notice to Vacate served. I hope we won't have to go through the ugly matter of an eviction."

"What the fuck," I say.

"It's for the best," he says.

"We didn't do anything wrong!" Erin says.

"I know," he says, "but it's complicated."

"This isn't right," I say.

"I know," he says, "but you see, Andy is my step-father. I mean—my mother's been dead for fifteen years, of course, but Andy and I have history."

"Oh," I say. "Now I see."

"So you're just going to let him get away with it," Erin says.

"I'm not letting him get away with anything."

"You condone his actions," I say.

"I *don't* condone what he did," Mr. Baumberger says angrily, looking at me now. "He'll be punished. He'll go to jail. But I can't evict him, this has been his home for a long time and he's an old man. If you two stay, he'll just do something stupid again, he'll want revenge. He's always been stubborn and vengeful, and I'm afraid what he might do. I won't charge you rent for the thirty days, but it would be easier for all of us if you find a new home."

* * * * * * *

Obviously I don't have the money to hire a lawyer, so I'm appointed a public defender.

I find myself sitting in my public defender's small office downtown. The office smells like mildew and there's files everywhere; the place is a mess.

My public defender looks younger than me and that doesn't help my self-esteem. I'm twenty-eight, I should have some kind of career by now. I should have an office. I should be able to hire a good defense lawyer. My court-appointed attorney, she has short blonde hair and wears glasses. I find myself sexually attracted to her.

She says, "Okay, so I spoke to the D.A.'s office, and this is what they're offering you. They want you to do some time," she says.

"What?" I say.

"Just listen now," she says. "Thirty days, but you won't actually do a month. You'll be in there, at most, fifteen days. Probably ten. Plus a year's probation; keep your nose clean for a year and you'll be fine. Actually," she smiles when she says this, "keep your nose clean for the rest of your life, and you'll be okay."

"It was self-defense," I say, softly.

"Yes, and it would be fun to try the case on that merit. But look: the man is very old, and small. The D.A. will ask: 'Could he really have done harm to this big young guy?' You can reject their offer, we can go to trial, but if for any reason we lose, you'll be facing six months to a year. You don't want that."

"No," I say, "I definitely don't want that."

"Look, I'll be honest," she says. "Your two prior convictions don't help. They're misdemeanors—petty theft and pubic intoxication—but they're on your record."

"I was eighteen," I say.

"You were an adult," she says, "they're on your record."

"So that old fart gets away with it."

"No, no, not at all. He's taking a plea: four months."

"That's all?"

She says, "He's an old man."

"Why does he get a break for his age?"

She says, "That's the way the system works. Look, we can get this over with. Do the time, make them happy. I'm not trying to pressure you into this decision. I'll be happy to take this to trial."

"Two weeks, maybe ten days," I say. "I guess that isn't too bad. It's not a year."

"Did you do any time for the other stuff?"

"I was in a holding cell for five days."

"And nothing bad happened?"

"It was boring," I tell her. "Time goes by slowly there."

"You don't have to make a decision right away," she says. "The D.A. can wait a few days."

"Call them now," I say. "The hell with it, I'll do the time."

"Are you sure?"

"No," I say, "but I don't want to go to trial, and I don't want to lose and get—what? Six months to a year?"

"I'm sorry you're in this situation," she says. "You can't even walk clean from self-defense these days. The Powers That Be want people to restrain themselves from any kind of violence, justified or not, so they wind up prosecuting the wrong people in the name of peace and security. I don't know what's happening to this country. These D.A.s can act like Nazis when they want to."

I ask, "So what will happen? When do I go to jail?"

"There'll be a court date in a week or so. You'll plead to the deal and be taken into the custody of the sheriff. You do your time, you go back home, you keep your nose clean, you put this silly mess behind you. Okay?" she says.

* * * * * * *

Erin is not happy. "You're going to go to *jail?*" she says. "Now isn't that just fucking great," she says.

"Fourteen days. Maybe ten."

"One day is a day too long," Erin says. "You're innocent," she laughs. "Doesn't that sound funny: 'You're innocent.'"

I try to touch her. She moves away from me.

"Here we are, we're being kicked out," she goes, "and you're leaving me."

"I'm not leaving you."

"I'll be alone."

"I won't be gone long."

"What if you die in there?"

"I won't die in there."

"What if you get raped?"

"That won't happen either."

She says, "You sound like you *want* to go to jail."

"That's crazy," I say. "I don't want to go to *trial*. Do you? Do you want to get up on the stand and have to be questioned?"

"I don't—I wish we didn't have to deal with any of this," she says.

"We don't have any choice."

"It seems like you don't."

She's standing by the window.

I say, "Erin."

She says, "What?"

"I'll be back before you know it."

She says, "I might not be here when you get out."

"You'll look for a new apartment?"

She stares out the window.

"What are you looking at?" I say.

"Birds," she says.

I stand next to her.

"I don't see any birds," I say.

"That's because you're not looking."

I touch her arm.

She says, "Don't."

"Why are you acting like this?"

"Why is there so much constant drama with us?" she says. "With you? Seems like every week it's one thing or another. I'm a nervous thing. All I want is peace, peace and quiet and enough money to go out to dinner and have a drink now and then. I never asked for much, and I never asked for this."

"What are you saying?"

"What I'm saying," she says; "I'm not saying anything."

"This will all be over soon," I say.

To that, she nods.

SHAME SCAM

1.

I had bad credit and this made me a target. The money in my checking account was disappearing like morning fog on a hot beach. I hadn't worked in three months because of a back injury I got while shooting a stunt. I'm a tinsel town stunt man, or I was, and I had an accident. My lawyer and I agreed on a settlement with the insurance company, but it was taking a while for the money to process.

"Unfortunately," my lawyer said on the phone, "the proverbial wheels move slow in this business."

"Can you grease the proverbials?" I asked.

"Wish I could," he said. "Look," he said, "the money will be here any day, eh."

With rent for my apartment in North Hollywood, food, the monthly minimum on my two maxed-out cards and other necessary bills, I figured in three months I'd be out on the street. I couldn't work because my back really did hurt and no film director in town would hire me until I was in the clear.

"Go on unemployment," my ex-girlfriend suggested one night.

"I can't," I told her, "I owe the state money."

"How's that?"

"Seven years ago I was getting unemployment, then I did a few jobs I didn't report. *They* eventually found out; twice a year I get a bill asking for the $1,225.56 I cheated the state out of."

My ex-girlfriend gave me this look, and she sighed. "Vern," she said, "you have to stop doing shit like that."

"Not now, okay?"

"And you wonder why I broke up with you," she said.

2.

Usually, when telemarketers call, I say no thanks and hang up, or just hang up. But not this time; the woman on the other end of the phone had a very nice voice, and at that moment—it was 10:30 in the morning—I needed to hear such a voice.

"Mr. Maddox? Mr. Vernon Maddox?"

"Yes?"

"May I call you Vern?"

I said, "Most people do."

She said, "Vern, I bet you could use some money right now. Vern, I bet a credit card would come in handy just about now. Am I right, or am I right?"

I said, "You're right."

"Well, then, I'm in a position to help you; the company I work for can help you. Yes, indeed, Vern, National Benefits Corp is the ticket for your ride."

"So," I said, "what's the scam?"

"Hey, this is no scam," she said. "We *can* help you."

"How?"

"We can give you a MasterCard."

"Look," I said.

"Vern," she said. "Please, hear me out. Won't you hear me out?"

"You'd be wasting your time."

"Give me two minutes, Vern. Can you give me two minutes?"

"Sure," I said.

"Your credit isn't so hot right now—that's why we have your number. Everyone working here at National Benefits Corp has been there; we know how it goes. So here's the offer: we can give you a MasterCard with a $1,500 credit limit. We have a one-time processing fee of $59.95 and an annual membership fee of $99.95. The one-time processing fee will be billed to your card the first month; the membership fee can also be billed that first month, or spread out over ten payments. Your choice. That's the key, Vern: it's all your choice. It's your life, your money, *you choose.*"

"That's almost $160," I said, "for $1,500 of credit?"

"I think it's a good deal, Vern. I mean, you can't sit there and tell me that you *don't* need $1,500—right now or anytime soon. Plus, every six months, you're eligible for a $500 credit increase."

"What's the finance charge?"

"19.5%," she said. "Waived if you pay your full month's balance each month before the due date."

All I could think of was my impending dire financial situation and how another card might be nice in case of an emergency. "What the hell," I said, "give it to me."

Her voice brightened even more: "A *good* choice, Vern. Now, I have to tell you, there's this big package I *have* to send you—some paperwork you need to fill out, some literature about everything we offer. To defray the printing and postage costs, there's a one-time charge of $9.95. We can take care of this via Check-By-Phone, and I'll have that package out to you this afternoon."

I gave her my checking account information—router number, account number, check number—which she quickly processed.

"On behalf on National Benefits Corp," she said, "I welcome you aboard."

"Hey, wait," I said.

"Yes?"

"What's your name?"

"Have a good day, sir."

3.

The package arrived two weeks later. I didn't bother to read all the promotional materials—like the specials I could get on air line tickets, hotels, restaurants and theater seats if I signed up—and they seemed to want just way too much personal information on the "paperwork." It was a waste of ten bucks; so I called the 888 number to cancel my possible membership.

"Why do you want to cancel?" the operator for National Benefits Corp asked me. Her voice was coarse and tired.

"I've decided that I'm not interested," I said.

"Why?"

"I'm just not."

"But why?"

"I don't have to tell you why."

"No you don't," she said, "but why don't you tell me anyway?"

"I don't want your damn card," I said.

"Why?"

"Would you stop asking me that!"

"Don't you *need* a credit card?"

"Actually, no."

"You were interested before."

"I wasn't thinking straight."

"Oh, *now*, Mr. Maddox, I *know* you can use this card."

"I don't want it."

"You don't sound sincere about that, Mr. Maddox."

"Look," I said, "are you going to cancel me or what? I don't want you to send me any more mail, and I don't want you to sell my address or phone number."

"Maybe you should sleep on this, Mr. Maddox," the operator said. "I'm sure you'll think differently in the morning."

I said, "Put me through to a supervisor."

"A supervisor? Why?"

"Just do it."

"Why would you want to talk to a supervisor, Mr. Maddox?"

"Because you're not being cooperative."

"Of *course* I am."

"You're not doing what I'm asking."

"What *are* you asking?"

"For you to cancel me from your system."

"Mr. Maddox, did you read about all the wonderful benefits you'd receive when you become a member?"

"Are you going to do what I say, or do I have to lodge some kind of complaint?"

"Why would you want to do that?"

"Listen, what's your name? What's your operator number?"

"Why do you want to know that, Mr. Maddox? You're being irrational."

I took a deep breath and told myself not to scream. "Look, you annoying bitch, cancel me out of your goddamn system."

"Very well, I will," she said, and hung up.

4.

But that wasn't the end of it. A week later, looking at my bank statement, I noticed three withdrawals attributed to "NBC" for $9.95, $59.95, and $99.95. I called my bank and told them I only authorized the first payment, not the other two.

"They're ACH payments," the bank person on the phone said. She kept sneezing as I talked to her.

"What's that?"

"Did you do a Check-By-Phone with this organization?"

"Yeah," I said softly.

"Unfortunately, these transactions are more than forty-eight hours old. We can get the money back if we're notified within two days; after that, you have to go to them."

"I see."

"This happens a lot," I was told. "You have to be careful about who you give your account information to. If you'd like, we can notify you if this happens again."

"Please," I said. Then I called National Benefits Corp. The operator was a male with a southern accent. I explained the situation to him. "I canceled," I said.

"I see that you did cancel, it's here on your account. But there's no record of these payments, other than the $9.95 for the membership package."

"I have a record right here, on my bank statement."

"It's not here."

"What's going on? Are you people trying to rip me off?"

"There must be some kind of mistake, sir."

"You bet there is."

"I can give you the corporate number if you'd like. You can talk to someone there."

"Please."

I called the corporate number and got voice mail. I left a message. For three days I left messages and no one returned my calls.

Then the bank called, informing me that NBC was attempting to make two ACH withdrawals: $59.95 and $99.95.

"Don't let them do it," I said.

"We can make a stop payment on these requests," I was told. "The fee will be $10."

I sighed.

"If you'd like," I was told, "we can put a permanent block on any future ACH requests from this company."

"What will it cost?"

"$15."

"Do it."

This is when things got *really* interesting.

5.

The first call from NBC came four days later, early in the morning. The man on the other end had a deep and serious voice. "Mr. Maddox," he said, "we have a bit of a problem."

"It's about time you people called. What's with stealing money from my bank account?"

"Yes, your bank account," he said. "You need to fix your bank account, Mr. Maddox."

"What?"

"You placed a block on your account. We have payments coming back, rejected. This isn't going to help your existing shabby credit history."

"You people took $160 out of my account, which I did *not* authorize."

"Of course you authorized it. You gave us the go ahead to enroll you in our program."

"All I wanted was to read your literature, and for that you got ten bucks out of me. I did *not* enroll, I did *not* want to be a member. You took two fees out, and I didn't even *get* a card."

"No, *our* attempts to collect the fees were met with rejection by *your* bank account."

"And not only did you take $160, you tried to take it *again*. Now tell me," I asked, "are you people thieves, or is there something wrong with your computers?"

"You entered a verbal deal with us over the phone," the man said, talking slowly, emphasizing each word, "and we expect you to honor it. And The Computer," he said with emphasis, "never makes mistakes."

"The fuck," I said. "You already got the money out of me. And what did I get? I don't want your card, I don't want your program. What I want, dude, is my goddamn money back."

"What we want," he said, "is the money you owe us."

"What do I have to do? Go to the authorities."

He laughed.

"You find that funny," I said.

"No wonder you have bad credit," he said. "You obviously have a problem with honoring debts."

"I'm going to ask you one more time," I said, "and I'm even going to ask you nicely. Would you please return the money you unlawfully removed from my bank account?"

"Mr. Maddox," he said, "I believe you fail to comprehend the gravity of this situation."

"What's your name?"

"You don't need to know my name."

"Yes I do. Who are you?"

"Someone you don't want to know too well, believe me."

"Is that a threat?"

"Mr. Maddox, I'm going to ask—no, I'm going to *tell* you something *once* and *only* once, and it is this: take the blockage of National Benefits Corp *off* your bank account."

I laughed, called him an ass, and hung up.

He phoned several hours later. He said, "Mr. Maddox, I hope you have come to your senses and have done what I asked."

"You didn't *ask*, you told me. Remember?"

He said, "Is the block off the account?"

I said, "Just who in the hell are you?"

"A nightmare for you," he said, and hung up.

I found the literature they sent me. The return address for NBC was a P.O. box in Hollywood, Florida. I shook my head and said to myself, "Florida." So when he called me again, early the next morning, I was ready for him. "Tell me," I asked, "how's the weather down there in Hollywood, Florida?"

He paused before responding. "What makes you think I'm in Florida?"

"That's where NBC is."

"That doesn't mean I'm there. Look, Mr. Maddox, if your intent is to intimidate me, it's not working."

"Oh, I forgot. *You're* the one who has the job to intimidate."

"Yes, you can look at it that way—"

"Is that your title?" I asked. "The Intimidator?"

"Listen, Mr. Maddox," he said, "you need to remove the block from your account."

"So you can steal more money from me?"

"You're viewing this whole matter in the wrong light."

"You listen to me, Mr. Whateveryournameis. I am going to the authorities. The cops there in Hollywood, the cops here in Hollywood; the FBI or the Florida attorney's general office—whoever it is I have to go to and file a criminal complaint, I will."

"You don't want to do that."

"No, I don't. So why don't you return my money, and I won't have to?"

"We don't owe you money," he said. "You know it's the other way around."

"What is it with you?" I said. "Do you want to go to jail?"

He chuckled—there was an echo. I pictured him in a big empty room, sitting at a desk with a phone or a head-set, wearing a cheap suit.

"I look forward to the day they bust you."

"Bust?" he said. *"I'm* going to bust your nose, Mr. Maddox. That's the only busting that's going to occur. I'm going to bust your nose open and show you a world of pain," and then the line went dead.

6.

He called at midnight. He spoke in a whisper: "You go to the authorities, you'll regret it."

"Maybe I already filed a complaint," I said, half-asleep.

"I don't think you did," he said, "but if you did, you are going to be very sorry."

"Do you know it's illegal to make these kind of threats?"

"You should be afraid; yes, yes you should. I could be there in L.A., you know. I *could* be watching you."

"But you're not."

"How do you know? We have people in L.A. We have people everywhere. We have people to *take care* of our business."

"I'm not afraid," I said.

"You should be," he said.

"Then come get me," I said.

"If I have to come to you," he said, "I will punch you in the brain."

7.

The next call:

"Yes, as I said before, I will punch you in the brain, Mr. Maddox."

"Listen," I said, "I don't even know what to call you. Here we are, we're speaking on such a regular basis, you know my name but what's yours? What kind of relationship is this?"

"You're not funny."

"I've always fancied myself a comedian."

"This is not a funny situation," he said. "This is fucking serious."

"Yes, it is serious," I said. "If you don't stop harassing me, I'll call the police."

"And then what? Will you get a restraining order on me? You don't know my name, Mr. Maddox, and you have no idea where I'm calling from."

"I know who you work for."

"They'll categorically deny it. Look, Mr. Maddox, *look:* there is a very simple way out of this predicament you have found yourself in. Remove the block from your bank account. Then we'll all be happy."

"So you people can steal $160 from me once a month?"

"A small price."

"What kind of strong-arming is this? What are you, some kind of phone Mafia?"

"Ah, the Mafia," he said. "What do the Mafia do, Mr. Maddox? They break legs, they break arms. They break faces. These are things that can happen to you."

"Like I said before, come get me."

8.

"Do you know what I can do to your life, Mr. Maddox?"

"Tell me."

"I could find your girlfriend and rape her."

"I don't have a girlfriend."

"Your boyfriend."

"Funny."

"You know what I mean."

"I don't. Tell me."

"People close to you—mom, dad, ex-girlfriend, best buddy. We have out ways; we can find someone, and we'll hurt this person."

"Maybe there isn't anyone I'm close to."

"If this is true, you are a sad, *sad* man."

9.

"You must be getting tired of my phone calls, Mr. Maddox."

"Actually, I've started to look forward to them."

"*I'm* getting tired of calling you. It seems to me we have to pay you a visit."

"I'll be here."

"We have guns."

"I'm shaking in my boots."

"MR. MADDOX, YOU WILL DO AS I TELL YOU!"

"Testy."

"YOU ARE A DEAD MAN!"

10.

The next call, he sounded drunk. "You fucker," he slurred. "You motherfucker. I hate you. I fucking hate you. Do you know much I stinking fucking HATE you?!"

11.

I changed my phone number and the calls stopped. I rang my lawyer to tell him about the change. My lawyer said, "Speak of the devil! I happen to have a check here for you; a very nice big check."

"You're kidding."

"It came this morning."

"I'll be right there."

I drove fast to his office.

I thought about asking him for advice on the National Benefits Corp problem, but I didn't feel he'd have any. Or he'd bill me an hour. I had a better idea anyway; it came to me in the car.

My lawyer asked, "So, now that you have your settlement, what will you do?"

"I'm going to take a vacation."

"Vacations are good."

"I'm going to Florida."

"Oh, I *love* Florida."

12.

The weather in Hollywood, Florida wasn't that different from Hollywood, California—there was less smog, of course, and the air was a little more moist and thick.

I got a rental car and checked into a motel in North Beach; my window revealed a nice view of the ocean and surfers catching waves.

I had a Plan A and a Plan B. Plan A was to apply for a job at National Benefits Corp; I figured that a telemarketing operation like that had high turnover and was always hiring desperate people in a need of a quick job. I'd done the telemarketing routine when I was younger. Plan B was to just go straight to the Post Office and hang out near their box, wait for someone to pick up the mail.

Plan A it was; I found an ad for the company in the help wanted section of the local newspaper. I called the number listed, talked to a tired-sounding fellow for a minute, and was given an appointment time the next morning.

The address was in a complex of business buildings—drab concrete gray structures. I was prompt for the appointment, and so were a dozen other people. It was a group thing, and the group consisted of men and women young and old—American, Cuban, and Haitian.

We were all "hired" within a half an hour—all we had to do was sign some paperwork; we'd be independent subcontractors being paid on commission. We'd receive minimum wage for a day's worth of training, which would be the next morning, and after that, we were on our own.

The next day was half a day, three hours at most. We were given a five-page script that we'd use when talking to people on the phone; there was the initial pitch and the answers to just about any question a potential victim might have.

I say "victim" because that's what the people on the other line—all across America—were. I was one, had been one. Everything about this operation was bullshit, I quickly spotted all the lies that I fell for and wondered how they got me in the first place.

Money.

The object, of course, was to get the bank account information from the people we'd call.

Did this organization actually issue credit cards? Supposedly. But it was not a phone operator's place to ponder such things. A phone operator sat at his or her station as The Computer dialed numbers.

13.

During the break, I sat outside on the hot concrete, eating an apple and drinking from a small carton of milk I purchased in the break room. Cost: $2.

A young lady with soft white skin sat next to me. She was very skinny and had crooked teeth. I liked her eyes. Her hair was long, dark and straight. She chewed on baby carrots.

She asked, "So, Holmes, what do you think?"

I said, "I think I'd rather be at the beach."

"I hear you," she said. "Man, it sucks needing a job."

I nodded.

She said, "You think the Feds might raid this place?"

"What do you mean?"

"You *know* what's going on here. All these places are alike."

I shrugged, trying to look dumb. I was undercover, after all.

She said, "Two months ago I was working a telemarketing gig across town. Buy three roll of films, you might win a vacation to Los Angeles. You know, go there and maybe you'll see the movie stars. Take pictures of them with your three rolls of film. I was there for *two* days and I go out for lunch, I go across the street to the Burger King, and I'm sitting in the B.K. eating a Whopper and I see all these black cars and vans swoop in and surround the place where I work. And I see all my supervisors and these people I work for being taken away in handcuffs. And that night I see on the news how the FBI cracked down on a telemarketing scam. Man, I was lucky I had that Whopper, or I would be in lock-up."

"It would make a great commercial for Burger King," I said. "'Aren't you happy you had a Whopper?'"

She smiled, exposing a lot of teeth pointing in various directions. "Yeah? Think so? Yeah. Cool."

14.

I started work the next day. I was given a head-set and a computer screen. Before I began, I was told that if I had a difficult potential customer, I would transfer the call to Super A, a woman with dreadlocks. If The Computer sent me a call from an existing customer with a complaint that I wasn't equipped to handle (I could only deal with certain questions, which my script had the answers to), I would transfer my call to Super B, a handsome fellow with long black hair in a pony tail.

The guy sitting at the computer screen next to me said, "Super B knows how to deal with the jerks. He's been here the longest."

The job wasn't in me, but I did my best. I talked to men and women and lied to them. I was on a mission, I played the part. I signed up two unsuspecting people in my first hour. $45 a person, I made $90 commission. I decided this was a good time to request a bathroom break. I really did have to go. I passed by Super B's office. His door was closed. He was talking to someone via his headset. I couldn't hear him. He was a tall, slender guy with dark skin, wearing a white shirt, a blue tie, and black slacks. I went to the restroom and took a piss. Coming back, Super B's door was cracked open. I could hear him when I walked by:

"Listen, Mrs. Dalrymple, we can ruin your credit. More than it's been ruined. It'll be destroyed for the rest of your life. Do you want that? *Do you?* Mrs. Dalrymple? *Stop* crying. Stop crying like a goddamn baby. *I hate that.* Now, you listen to me. You do what I say. Okay? *Okay?* Okay, *now* we're talking. *Now* we're being reasonable, Mrs. Dalrymple."

It was him.

It was his voice.

15.

I sat at my post, wondering how I'd do this.

I'd just do it. I didn't want to be here a minute longer. I was here for one reason only.

I got up, headed straight for Super B's office, closed and locked his door, and said, "Hey."

He was talking into his headset, then stopped.

I said, "Hang up."

He just looked at me.

I reached over at pulled the headset out of the phone-jack.

"What the—"

I smiled.

"What the fuck," he said. "What the *fuck* is your malfunction, buddy boy?"

I socked him in the nose. There was blood. He tried to make it for the door. I grabbed him by the pony tail and slammed his face into his desk.

"So we meet at last," I said.

"What the hell do you think you're doing?" he said.

"Don't you recognize my voice?" I asked.

"What?"

"I'm going to let you up," I said. "If you try anything funny, I will punch you in the brain. Oh yes, you *know* that phrase well. *I will punch your brain, asshole."*

I released him, taking a step back.

He touched his nose and looked at the blood on his fingers. "You can't do this to me," he said. "I'm a Seminole Indian."

"My name is Vern," I said, "Vernon Maddox."

It took him a moment. The color went out of his face. I liked how white he suddenly became, a true pale face.

He said, "No shit."

I said, "Oh yeah."

He said, "You want payback."

I said, "And I'm about to get it."

I was ready for a fight. He seemed fit. Instead, he screamed. His scream was quite up there in the decibels. His scream hurt my ears. He jumped up on his desk and cried for help. I tried to grab his legs. He leapt for the door. He ran out the door, shrieking. I went after him. It was like an old Keystone Cops flick as I chased him around the many confused and bemused phone operators. I chased him out the building. He got into his car—a Honda Civic—and sped away from the parking lot. I got into my rental and contemplated a pursuit. He was long gone, and it was now time for me to go home.

16.

The next day I called the administrative line to National Benefits Corp. A computerized voice said: "If you know your party's three-digit extension, you may dial at any time."

I knew his extension all right, *Mr. Super B.*

He was there.

He said, "Hello."

I said, "How's the nose, buddy?"

Silence.

"Hello?" I said.

"What?" he said.

"It's your favorite dude—me: Mr. Maddox. What do you have to say now?"

"You're in big trouble," he said softly, "you don't know who you just messed with. You're in a world of pain, a universe of double trouble, pal. *I'm* a Seminole Indian."

"And I'm a professional stuntman," I said. "The guy who's in the shit is you, my friend. Because I know *where you work*. And I know *where you live*. Yes, I know where your crib is, homeboy. I followed you when you high-tailed it out in your piece of shit Honda like some scared little bitch. You *hear* me, *bitch?* You're the one who's about to get punched in the brain."

He hung up.

17.

When I returned to Los Angeles, I dialed Florida from an airport payphone. Super B. didn't answer his extension. I was routed to an operator: "How may I direct your call?"

I *still* didn't know the guy's name. "I'm trying to reach Super B."

"Oh," I was told, "he doesn't work here anymore."

SHAME GODDESS

1.

Give my Goddess my money, all my money and whatever she demands, whatever she wishes, because I am hers and she is mine and it took me a long time and many false tries to find her, so that we could both be happy; it does not matter if I have never seen her in the real world, that her flesh has never touched mine either gently or in anger—our love does not need the mundane aspects of the body; it is the connection of our minds, and the exchange of energy—money—that forms the basis of our relationship.

2.

Let me explain now it started with me, this need to give women money. First, it's something I always fantasized about: a certain scenario, and when I encountered Suzy online, I had the opportunity to act out my fantasy. Her profile at OurSpace popped when I typed in the search term "money slave." On her profile: "Interested in meeting money slaves of all kinds. I can be your mistress!" She lived in Los Angeles as I did. I liked her profile photos: she had dark hair, wore her make-up Goth style; pale skin, large breasts, a devious glint in her dark blue eyes. If she had been there in the flesh, I would have opened my wallet and given her everything I had: $250 and three credit cards, each with a $3,000 limit.

I wrote Suzy and told her I was a money slave and would love to give her $50 if she was interested in meeting and acting out a scenario. She wrote back that she would indeed. I was floored. Here is our correspondence:

From: Me
To: Suzy

Whoa! Yikes, that is. You replied. Um, non-irately Sorry. Seriously. It was an irrepressible impulse. I am completely, utterly profilesmitten. Um, would you, honestly, seriously, Ms Suzy? That is so gratuitously cool and kind and generous and open of you! I'm not sure what to say or ask next. Sorry. I'm feeling a bit flushed and fevery-like suddenly. Something about your profile photo hovering above your bewitchingly brief and to-the-chase reply is making me all nervous a babbly. I hope this actually happens. I suppose I could say that I live in Santa Monica...but that wouldn't be to imply that I wouldn't travel to Kirkuk to meet you, if those were your terms. Thanks for your reply in any event. That was really kind. And sort of an enormous thrill, I actually.

From: Suzy
To: Me

Somewhere public for sure, since you could be a psycho killer or something. You really have a fetish for this kind of thing? That is so very interesting. I wrote that I wanted to meet money slaves as a joke, sort of, but didn't think it'd ever happen.

From: Me
To: Suzy

Hooray! I'm dizzy with my good luck. I'm so glad I finally plucked up the audacity to add you! And, yes, it is an actual fetish. But, I hasten to add, one that I find as hilarious and ridiculous as you surely must.

Unfortunately, I also happen to find intensely erotic. When are you available to try this, Suzy? I will turn my life upside down to accommodate you. You really need only to tell me to give you $50, take it, and walk away. I'll meet you anywhere you prefer. Somewhere coffee-ish, somewhere booze-ish, or just a corner with an ATM.

Thank you over and over infinitely for this!

From: Suzy
To: Me

Awesome. Well, there's some birthday thing that's happening either Friday or Saturday. Hmm. I could meet Friday, and if the birthday thing happens, I could just go to that afterward. Wow, I feel almost bad about taking money and walking away; you seem like a nice guy—but hey, if that's what gets you off, cool. I don't mind having a beer and chatting though, unless that's weird for you.

From: Me
To: Suzy

Having an actual conversation (however humiliated and tongue-tied) with someone so absurdly, impossibly WOW!!! would be my life's crowning moment, Suzy. But I'm not sure I can rely on that much courage. It took me an hour of nerve-rallying just to click your friend add button from the safety of my own home But it will be a gigantic honor to meet you Friday. And it will be a gigantic thrill to give you $50 for, well, being absurdly, impossibly WOW!!! And, hopefully, hopefully, it will be the first of several decreasingly terrifying similar meetings. Thanks inexpressibly. I know I keep saying that, but I keep meaning it.

From: Suzy
To: Me

Okay, whatever you're most comfortable with. I don't
want to freak you out, although I'm not a scary or in-
timidating person at all. What time is good for you? I
usually get home by 6, so I could get ready and be
there by 8pm.

To: Suzy
From: Me
This sounds perfectly perfect! I'll actually have to do
a wee bit of plan rearranging (which I couldn't be
more thrilled and elated to do.) If by some unlikely
miracle of fortune you still exist when I wake up tomorrow and I haven't dreamed this entire exchange,
I will make calls and write you to confirm. And then
stumble about in a blissful daze until 8 PM Friday.

Yes, that's what I wanted, what I desired: for a woman, a stranger, a
beautiful or cute woman—maybe *any* woman—to come up to me in
a public space and demand $50 from me. She might say, "I'm pretty
so give me $50" because her good looks demand monetary compen-
sation. Or just, "Give me $50." I will do as she commands; if she
asks for more, I will give her more, I will give her everything, I
might even walk to an ATM and take out my daily limit. I am not a
wealthy man, I cannot give a demanding goddess hundreds of dollars, or thousands, as much as I wish I could. I am on a budget and
$50 seems about right to break the ice; we could up the ante if the
relationship continued.

I was terrified, if that doesn't come across. I do not do well in
the real world with women, and was horrified of any woman knowing about my secret need. It was hard enough to express this
online—and now it was going to happen? Was it really going to
happen?

3.

We agreed upon a restaurant in West Hollywood, a trendy place where good-looking people converged, where there were lots of people to witness. You see, part of the scenario in my mind is that a few people would witness this interaction, would observe me humiliated, would gaze on me and say to themselves, "Look at that poor pussy-whipped sap, he just caves in and gives that demanding bitch the money." Yes! I want them to pity me, to see me as dirt, a man who allows women to walk all over him, abuse him, make him poor.

I waited in the bar area of the restaurant, sipping on a beer. I was very nervous. I didn't know if she would show up or not. She was only one minute late. I recognized her from her online picture: that hair, that skin. She wore a tight yellow leather mini-skirt and a white blouse. She looked magnificent and I was excited by the fact that other men had taken notice of her, but she was here for me.

I did not have an online photo but I told her I would be at the bar wearing jeans, a blue shirt, and a black blazer, and that I wore dark-rimmed glasses and my hair was shoulder-length and blonde.

She spotted me. I made like I did not know she was there: I casually sipped my beer and looked the other way.

A tap on my shoulder. "Hey."

I turned.

She glared. "Give me fifty bucks, you."

I was trembling, slightly. I reached for my wallet. I took two twenty dollar bills and two five dollar bills and handed them to her.

She said nothing else, per script. She took the money with a little nod and walked away. I watched her rear end sway back and forth with haughty triumph and I think I fell in love. She left the restaurant and that was that.

Three people at the bar had witnessed and took notice of the exchange. They gave me quick funny looks, then went back to their business.

4.

I was so shaken and delirious that I could not drive back home. I took a taxi. The taxi could not get there fast enough. Once in, I pulled my pants down and jerked off, thinking about her. It happened fast. The second time, I looked at her image online, imagining that I was handing over hundred dollar bills.

5.

Our second encounter was at a small bar on Sunset Boulevard and Highland Avenue. Another trendy spot with trendy people to see it happen. This time she said, "I'm pretty so give me $50." Yes, she was pretty, wearing a black dress that clung nicely to her form.

Our third encounter was at a small coffee shop on Melrose, one known to be a favorite among TV actors. "I'm hot and I deserve $50," she demanded. I had a crisp fifty dollar with Benjamin Franklin's smiling visage for her.

6.

I didn't have a name for what I was, not at first, but others did: paypigs, money pigs, financial pigs, payrobots, money sluts, cashcows, human ATM machines. These words send tingles up my spine and caused a stirring in my loins.

I did my initial research online. *Financial domination* has two essential elements: the "financial slave" interested in having a Money Dom or Money Mistress (sometimes Queen or Princess or Goddess) abuse and "ruin" his bank account, savings, and paycheck, and the Money Mistress who receives "tributes" in the form of bank wire transfers, money sent via PayPal or another online system, cash in the mail or in person, the payment of bills, and expensive gifts such as jewelry or clothing. On one website, Goddess M. stated the following under the category "You":

You might still be asking yourself what does Goddess M. expect from her money slaves, paypigs, and cashcows.

Since you have already read the rules, you understand that honesty is a major issue. As a submissive Worshipping male you Mr. Paypig eagerly accept My Greatness, and your role as my slave.

I expect my slave to be loyal, educated, financially successful, witty, open minded, and intellectual. I would prefer not to be embarrassed while seen with you. Even though I will be... Presentation does mean everything. You must know how to represent yourself

She provided a link, "Apply to be my money slave." She wrote on her website:

"Serving is about making ME happy, not about your kinky fantasies or YOUR needs! I am seeking a serious sub to spoil me. Financial control empowers me and puts you in your place... at my feet. I also offer keyholder service. So many approach this Mistress, a gift or tribute makes one stand out in the crowd."

Another money mistress with a vicious bent when it comes to her slave:

"I am a beautiful 23-year-old college student who loves to humiliate men and they worship me and drain their bank accounts in my honor. I have expensive tastes, and there is no limit to the amount of money I might demand. Whether you are a millionaire, or a regular joe, rest assured that I could reduce you to poverty."

Some mistresses offered items of clothing for tributes, such as underwear, socks, and stockings. One wrote:

"I have already mailed 5 pairs of stockings to different slaves. Those filthy animals are probably enjoying my feminine scent right now. Feeling the texture of them. Wearing them on their own legs and wishing they were really my legs.

I told one slave he should wear them under his pants and feel what it's like to have them clinging to his legs. The tight feeling of his balls being chafed when he goes to sit down. I told him to imagine that feeling was me squeezing his sack. He'll be sending pictures to me soon. I can't wait to see the filthy little worm in my stockings. It will be quite enjoyable."

In another blog, she posted a photo of herself holding a new mini-laptop with the caption: "I am now your net book Mistress, thanks to my wonderful Voiceslave who helped tribute to my new HP 2133 mini-computer!"

7.

All this new information was titillating beyond belief. I did not feel so alone in the world; I had no idea there were other men like me, with the same needs and fantasies. I told Suzy this in an email and she replied, "Didn't you know? Wow, you do have much to learn." *Teach me, teach me,* I wanted to write back, but was too afraid. For our next exchange, she made a bold move, one that I approved, telling me I would have to pay her $100 now, because of inflation and the shaky economy, "$50 isn't worth $50 anymore." So that's what happened. For our fifth encounter, however, she had a surprise for me, one that I was not prepared for, as it went off-script.

8.

Suzy chose the place: the Hustler Club. She said it was one of her favorite stores. Two days later, I was in the Hustler Club, shy and embarrassed to be in a place that sold videos and fetish items. But I was aroused as well.

There were a couple of customers in the store, and in an adjacent room, a dozen or so people sat in chairs and listened to a woman in a pink dress read some kind of erotic story: "He took out the whip and I knew I was going to get the beating of my life, the beating that would finally bring me happiness," she said in a soft voice.

I was not prepared for Suzy's attire this time: she entered the store in leather pants and a leather halter, high heel boots, her hair pulled back into a tight pony-tail. Her make-up was dark and extra-gothy. Her heels clacked as she walked toward me. My mouth was dry. I readied myself.

"You," she said, "it's time for a change. Things are going to be different now."

I was shocked.

"It will cost you *more* from now on," she said, "because I'm your Goddess, and I deserve everything you have."

"Y-yes," I stuttered, "y-you d-d-do."

"How much money do you have on you, walletworm?"

"O-one hundred," I said. I took the five twenty dollar bills out and handed them to her.

"Not enough, you worthless little piggy."

"I-I'm s-s-sorry."

She grabbed me by the shirt. "First, let's get out of here, *now.*"

She pushed me out the door.

"That way."

She pushed me down the street. We stopped at an ATM machine.

"Whip it out, *now.*"

I asked, "H-h-how mu-much?"

"What's your limit?"

"$300."

"Get to it, paypig."

Shaking, I put my ATM card into the machine. I only had $500 in my account, set aside for bills. Her taking the $300 would cause me to go in the whole. I could feel myself getting hard thinking about that.

I took the money out, and turned to her.

"On your knees."

I got on my knees, slowly.

"Your tribute," she said, "to your Goddess."

I held out the money. My voice was steady now: "Please take it, my Goddess, my love, as a token of my devotion to your beauty."

The words were alien in my mouth, but they the words I yearned all my life to say to a woman.

Suzy—Goddess Suzy, I should say—smiled. She took the money. She was $400 richer.

"Get up, *now.*"

I stood on my feet, slowly.

She grabbed my shirt again. "Let's go."

"Where?" I asked.

"Home," she said.

ABOUT THE AUTHOR

MICHAEL HEMMINGSON spends his time between Los Angeles and San Diego. His first feature film, *The Watermelon*, was released on DVD and Blu-Ray in 2009 from LightSong Films and Celebrity Video Distributors. He directed and narrated a short documentary, *Life in Zona Norte*, for Real Ideas Studio, which screened at the 2009 Cannes Film Festival. He has published some novels, short story collections, and edited a handful of anthologies, from *The Mammoth Book of Legal Thrillers* (2001) to *What the Fuck: The Avant-Porn Anthology* (2000). *Sexy Strumpet and Troublesome Trollops* is the second volume in a trilogy of erotic short stories for The Borgo Press/Wildside Press, the first being *How to Have an Affair and Other Instructions* (2007). The third volume will be called *Vexatious Vixens and Trailer Park Tramps*.

www.ingramcontent.com/pod-product-compliance
Lightning Source LLC
Chambersburg PA
CBHW031128210626
46816CB00015B/1233